# E. Nesbit

E(dith) NESBIT was born in London in 1858 and went to school in Europe. She was a mischievous, daring tomboy, and her escapades with her brothers and sisters in the countryside of Kent, England, inspired many of the adventures in her stories for young readers. Her literary career began at age fifteen with the sale of some poems to a magazine. When she was twenty-one, she married Hubert Bland, a socialist writer. The marriage was stormy and filled with scandal, and the family was usually poor. Still, their home was a favorite gathering place for writers and political activists.

Temperamental and independent, Edith Nesbit was a woman ahead of her time. She wore her hair cut short, smoked in public, and cared little for social conventions. She wrote constantly to support her growing family, grinding out countless stories and poems. In the late 1890s she began writing stories about children, which were an immediate success. Her Bastable family tales, *The Story of the Treasure Seekers, The Wouldbegoods,* and *The New Treasure Seekers,* were a fresh delight, for they were among the first ever written that did not preach. More books soon followed, including *The Railway Children* and the three books of Psammead stories: *Five Children and It, The Phoenix and the Carpet,* and *The Story of the Amulet.* Nesbit's skillful blending of fantasy and realism, liberally spiced with humor, served as a model for many later writers.

Hubert Bland died in 1914, and Edith Nesbit later married an old friend, with whom she enjoyed a much happier life until her death in 1924.

YEARLING CLASSICS

Works of lasting literary merit by English
and American classic and contemporary writers

HANS BRINKER, OR THE SILVER SKATES, *Mary Mapes Dodge*
EIGHT COUSINS, OR THE AUNT HILL, *Louisa May Alcott*
FIVE LITTLE PEPPERS AND HOW THEY GREW, *Margaret Sidney*
THE MIDNIGHT FOLK, *John Masefield*
FIVE CHILDREN AND IT, *E. Nesbit*
THE PRINCE AND THE PAUPER, *Mark Twain*
THE PRINCESS AND THE GOBLIN, *George MacDonald*
ROSE IN BLOOM, *Louisa May Alcott*
TOM'S MIDNIGHT GARDEN, *Philippa Pearce*
LITTLE LORD FAUNTLEROY, *Frances Hodgson Burnett*
THE BOOK OF DRAGONS, *E. Nesbit*
REBECCA OF SUNNYBROOK FARM, *Kate Douglas Wiggin*
A GIRL OF THE LIMBERLOST, *Gene Stratton Porter*
DOCTOR DOLITTLE: A TREASURY, *Hugh Lofting*
THE RETURN OF THE TWELVES, *Pauline Clarke*
FOUR DOLLS, *Rumer Godden*
THE PRINCESS AND CURDIE, *George MacDonald*
POLLYANNA, *Eleanor H. Porter*
FIVE LITTLE PEPPERS MIDWAY, *Margaret Sidney*

YEARLING BOOKS are designed especially to entertain and
enlighten young people. Charles F. Reasoner, Professor
Emeritus of Children's Literature and Reading, New York
University, is consultant to this series.

For a complete listing of all Yearling titles, write to
Dell Publishing Co., Inc., Promotion Department,
P.O. Box 3000, Pine Brook, N.J. 07058.

# The Phoenix and the Carpet

## E. Nesbit

### *With an Afterword by Susan Cooper*

To
my dear godson,
Hubert Griffith,
and
his sister,
Margaret

---

Published by
Dell Publishing Co., Inc.
1 Dag Hammarskjold Plaza
New York, New York 10017

Yearling ® TM 913705, Dell Publishing Co., Inc.

ISBN: 0-440-47035-8

RL: 6.0

Printed in the United States of America

February 1987

10 9 8 7 6 5 4 3 2 1

W

# To Hubert

Dear Hubert, if I ever found
A wishing carpet lying round,
I'd stand upon it, and I'd say:
"Take me to Hubert, right away!"
And then we'd travel very far
To where the magic countries are
That you and I will never see,
And choose the loveliest gifts for you, from me.

But oh! alack! and well-a-day!
No wishing carpets come my way.
I never found a Phoenix yet,
And Psammeads are so hard to get!
So I can give you nothing fine
Only this book, your book and mine,
And hers, whose name by yours is set;
Your book, my book, the book of Margaret!

E. Nesbit

Dymchurch,
    *September* 1904

# Contents

# Chapter 1

# The Egg

*I*t began with the day when it was almost the Fifth of November, and a doubt arose in some breast—Robert's, I fancy—as to the quality of the fireworks laid in for the Guy Fawkes celebration.

"They were jolly cheap," said whoever it was, and I think it was Robert, "and suppose they didn't go off on the night? Those Prosser kids would have something to snigger about then."

"The ones *I* got are all right," Jane said. "I know they are, because the man at the shop said they were worth thribble the money—"

"I'm sure thribble isn't grammar," Anthea said.

"Of course it isn't," said Cyril. "One word can't be grammar all by itself, so you needn't be so jolly clever."

Anthea was rummaging in the corner drawers of her mind for a very disagreeable answer, when she remembered what a wet day it was, and how the boys had been disappointed of that ride to London and back on the top of the tram, which their mother had promised them as a reward for not having once forgotten, for six whole days, to wipe their boots on the mat when they came home from school.

So Anthea only said, "Don't be so jolly clever yourself, Squirrel. And the fireworks look all right, and you'll have the eightpence that your tram fares didn't cost today to buy something more with. You ought to get a perfectly lovely Catherine wheel for eightpence."

"I daresay," said Cyril coldly. "But it's not *your* eightpence anyhow—"

"But look here," said Robert. "Really now, about the fireworks. We don't want to be disgraced before those kids next door. They think because they wear red plush on Sundays no one else is any good."

"I wouldn't wear plush if it was ever so—unless it was black to be beheaded in, if I was Mary Queen of Scots," said Anthea with scorn.

Robert stuck steadily to his point. One great point about Robert is the steadiness with which he can stick.

"I think we ought to test them," he said.

"You young duffer," said Cyril. "Fireworks are like postage stamps. You can only use them once."

"What do you suppose it means by 'Carter's tested seeds' in the advertisement?"

There was a blank silence. Then Cyril touched his forehead with his finger and shook his head.

"A little wrong here," he said. "I was always afraid of that with poor Robert. All that cleverness, you know, and being top in algebra so often—it's bound to tell—"

"Dry up," said Robert fiercely. "Don't you see? You can't *test* seeds if you do them *all*. You just take a few here and there, and if those grow you can feel pretty sure the others

will be—what do you call it?—Father told me—'up to sample.' Don't you think we ought to sample the fireworks? Just
shut our eyes and each draw one out, and then try them."

"But it's raining cats and dogs," said Jane.

"And Queen Anne is dead," rejoined Robert. No one was
in a very good temper. "We needn't go out to do them; we
can just move back the table, and let them off on the old tea
tray we play toboggans with. I don't know what *you* think,
but *I* think it's time we did something, and that would be
really useful; because then we shouldn't just *hope* the fireworks would make those Prossers sit up—we should *know*."

"It *would* be something to do," Cyril owned with languid
approval.

So the table was moved back. And then the hole in the
carpet, which had been near the window till the carpet was
turned round, showed most awfully. But Anthea stole out on
tiptoe, and got the tray when Cook wasn't looking, and
brought it in and put it over the hole.

Then all the fireworks were put on the table, and each of
the four children shut its eyes very tight and put out its hand
and grasped something. Robert took a cracker, Cyril and
Anthea had Roman candles; but Jane's fat paw closed on the
gem of the whole collection, the Jack-in-the-box that had
cost two shillings, and one at least of the party—I will not
say which, because it was sorry afterward—declared that
Jane had done it on purpose. Nobody was pleased. For the
worst of it was that these four children, with a very proper
dislike of anything even faintly bordering on the sneakish,
had a law, unalterable as those of the Medes and Persians,
that one had to stand by the results of a toss-up, or a drawing

of lots, or any other appeal to chance, however much one might happen to dislike the way things were turning out.

"I didn't mean to," said Jane, near tears. "I don't care, I'll draw another—"

"You know jolly well you can't," said Cyril bitterly. "It's settled. It's Medium and Persian. You've done it, and you'll have to stand by it—and us too, worse luck. Never mind. *You'll* have your pocket money before the fifth. Anyway, we'll have the Jack-in-the-box *last*, and get the most out of it we can."

So the cracker and the Roman candles were lighted, and they were all that could be expected for the money; but when it came to the Jack-in-the-box, it simply sat in the tray and laughed at them, as Cyril said. They tried to light it with paper and they tried to light it with matches; they tried to light it with Vesuvian fuses from the pocket of Father's second-best overcoat that was hanging in the hall. And then Anthea slipped away to the cupboard under the stairs where the brooms and dustpans were kept, and the rosiny firelighters that smell so nice and like the woods where pine trees grow, and the old newspapers, and the beeswax and turpentine, and the horrid stiff dark rags that are used for cleaning brass and furniture, and the paraffin for the lamps. She came back with a little pot that had once cost sevenpence-halfpenny when it was full of red currant jelly; but the jelly had been all eaten long ago, and now Anthea had filled the jar with paraffin. She came in, and she threw the paraffin over the tray just at the moment when Cyril was trying with the twenty-third match to light the Jack-in-the-box. The Jack-in-the-box did not catch fire any more than usual, but the paraffin acted quite differently, and in an instant a hot flash of flame leapt up and burnt off Cyril's eyelashes and scorched the faces of all four before they could spring back. They backed, in four instantaneous bounds, as far as they could, which was to the wall, and the pillar of fire reached from floor to ceiling.

"My hat," said Cyril with emotion, "you've done it this time, Anthea."

The flame was spreading out under the ceiling like the rose of fire in Mr. Rider Haggard's exciting story about Allan Quatermain. Robert and Cyril saw that no time was to be lost. They turned up the edges of the carpet and kicked them over the tray. This cut off the column of fire, and it disappeared and there was nothing left but smoke and a dreadful smell of lamps that have been turned too low. All hands now rushed to the rescue, and the paraffin fire was only a bundle of trampled carpet, when suddenly a sharp crack beneath their feet made the amateur firemen start back. Another crack—the carpet moved as if it had had a coat wrapped in it; the Jack-in-the-box had at last allowed itself to be lighted, and it was going off with desperate violence inside the carpet.

Robert, with the air of one doing the only possible thing, rushed to the window and opened it. Anthea screamed, Jane burst into tears, and Cyril turned the table wrong way up on top of the carpet heap. But the firework went on, banging and bursting and spluttering even underneath the table.

Next moment Mother rushed in, attracted by the howls of Anthea, and in a few moments the firework desisted and there was a dead silence, and the children stood looking at each other's black faces and, out of the corners of their eyes, at Mother's white one.

The fact that the nursery carpet was ruined occasioned but little surprise, nor was anyone really astonished that bed should prove the immediate end of the adventure. It has been said that all roads lead to Rome; this may be true, but at any rate, in early youth I am quite sure that many roads lead to *bed*, and stop there—or *you* do.

The rest of the fireworks were confiscated, and Mother was not pleased when Father let them off himself in the back garden, though he said, "Well, how else can you get rid of them, my dear?"

You see, Father had forgotten that the children were in disgrace and that their bedroom windows looked out on to the back garden. So that they all saw the fireworks most beautifully, and admired the skill with which Father handled them.

Next day all was forgotten and forgiven; only the nursery had to be deeply cleaned (like spring cleaning), and the ceiling had to be whitewashed.

And Mother went out; and just at teatime next day a man came with a rolled-up carpet, and Father paid him, and Mother said:

"If the carpet isn't in good condition, you know, I shall expect you to change it." And the man replied, "There ain't a thread gone in it nowhere, mum. It's a bargain, if ever there was one, and I'm more'n 'arf sorry I let it go at the price; but we can't resist the lydies, can we, sir?" and he winked at Father and went away.

Then the carpet was put down in the nursery, and sure enough there wasn't a hole in it anywhere.

As the last fold was unrolled something hard and loud-sounding bumped out of it and trundled along the nursery floor. All the children scrambled for it, and Cyril got it. He took it to the gaslight. It was shaped like an egg, very yellow and shiny, half transparent, and it had an odd sort of light in it that changed as you held it in different ways. It was as though it was an egg with a yolk of pale fire that just showed through the stone.

"I *may* keep it, mayn't I, Mother?" Cyril asked. And of course Mother said no; they must take it back to the man who had brought the carpet, because she had only paid for a carpet, and not for a stone egg with a fiery yolk to it.

So she told them where the shop was, and it was in the Kentish Town Road, not far from the hotel that is called the Bull and Gate. It was a poky little shop and the man was arranging furniture outside on the pavement very cunningly, so that the more broken parts should show as little as possible. And directly he saw the children he knew them again, and he began at once, without giving them a chance to speak.

"No, you don't," he cried loudly, "I aint' a-goin' to take back no carpets, so don't you make no bloomin' errer. A bargain's a bargain, and the carpet's puffik throughout."

"We don't want you to take it back," said Cyril. "But we found something in it."

"It must have got into it up at your place, then," said the man with indignant promptness, "for there ain't nothing in nothing as I sell. It's all as clean as a whistle."

"I never said it wasn't *clean*," said Cyril, "but—"

"Oh, if it's *moths*," said the man, "that's easy cured with borax. But I expect it was only an odd one. I tell you the carpet's good through and through. It hadn't got no moths when it left my 'ands—not so much as an hegg."

"But that's just it," interrupted Jane, "there *was* so much as an egg."

The man made a sort of rush at the children and stamped his foot.

"Clear out, I say," he shouted. "Or I'll call for the police. A nice thing for customers to 'ear you a-coming 'ere a-charging me with finding things in goods what I sells. 'Ere, be off, afore I sends you off with a flea in your ears. Hi! constable—"

The children fled, and they think, and their father thinks, that they couldn't have done anything else. Mother has her own opinion. But Father said they might keep the egg.

"The man certainly didn't know the egg was there when he brought the carpet," said he, "any more than your mother did, and we've as much right to it as he had."

So the egg was put on the mantelpiece, where it quite brightened up the dingy nursery. The nursery was dingy, because it was a basement room, and its windows looked out on a stone area with a rockery made of clinkers facing the windows. Nothing grew in the rockery except London pride and snails.

The room had been described in the house agent's list as a "convenient breakfast room in basement," and in the day-time it was rather dark. This did not matter so much in the evenings when the gas was alight, but then it was in the evening that the blackbeetles got so sociable, and used to come out of the low cupboards on each side of the fireplace where their homes were, and try to make friends with the children. At least, I suppose that was what they wanted, but the children never would.

On the fifth of November Father and Mother went to the theater, and the children were not happy, because the Prossers next door had lots of fireworks and they had none.

They were not even allowed to have a bonfire in the garden.

"No more playing with fire, thank you" was Father's answer, when they asked him.

When the baby had been put to bed the children sat sadly round the fire in the nursery.

"I'm beastly bored," said Robert.

"Let's talk about the Psammead," said Anthea, who generally tried to give the conversation a cheerful turn.

"What's the good of *talking?*" said Cyril. "What I want is for something to happen. It's awfully stuffy for a chap not to be allowed out in the evenings. There's simply nothing to do when you've got through your homers."

Jane finished the last of her home lessons and shut the book with a bang.

"We've got the pleasure of memory," said she. "Just think of last holidays."

Last holidays, indeed, offered something to think of—for they had been spent in the country at a white house between a sandpit and a gravel pit, and things had happened. The children had found a Psammead, or sand fairy, and it had let them have anything they wished for—just exactly anything, with no bother about its not being really for their good, or anything like that. And if you want to know what kind of things they wished for, and how their wishes turned out you can read it all in a book called *Five Children and It* (*It* was the Psammead). If you've not read it, perhaps I ought to tell you that the fifth child was the baby brother, who was called the Lamb, because the first thing he ever said was "Baa!" and that the other children were not particularly handsome, nor were they extra clever, nor extraordinarily good. But they were not bad sorts on the whole; in fact, they were rather like you.

"I don't want to think about the pleasures of memory," said Cyril. "I want some more things to happen."

"We're very much luckier than anyone else, as it is," said Jane. "Why, no one else ever found a Psammead. We ought to be grateful."

"Why shouldn't we *go on* being, though?" Cyril asked. "Lucky, I mean, not grateful. Why's it all got to stop?"

"Perhaps something will happen," said Anthea comfortably. "Do you know, sometimes I think we are the sort of people that things *do* happen to."

"It's like that in history," said Jane. "Some kings are full of interesting things, and others—nothing ever happens to them, except their being born and crowned and buried, and sometimes not that."

"I think Panther's right," said Cyril. "I think we are the sort of people things do happen to. I have a sort of feeling things would happen right enough if we could only give them a shove. It just wants something to start it. That's all."

"I wish they taught magic at school." Jane sighed. "I believe if we could do a little magic it might make something happen."

"I wonder how you begin?" Robert looked round the room, but he got no ideas from the faded green curtains, or the drab Venetian blinds, or the worn brown oilcloth on the floor. Even the new carpet suggested nothing, though its pattern was a very wonderful one, and always seemed as though it were just going to make you think of something.

"I could begin right enough," said Anthea. "I've read lots about it. But I believe it's wrong in the Bible."

"It's only wrong in the Bible because people wanted to hurt other people. I don't see how things can be wrong unless they hurt somebody, and we don't want to hurt anybody, and what's more, we jolly well couldn't if we tried. Let's get the *Ingoldsby Legends*. There's a thing about Abracadabra there," said Cyril, yawning. "We may as well play on magic. They used to work spells or something with a goat or a goose. Father says so."

"Well, that's all right," said Robert unkindly. "You can play the goat right enough, and Jane knows how to be a goose."

"I'll get *Ingoldsby*," said Anthea hastily. "You turn up the hearthrug."

So they traced strange figures on the linoleum, on the part where the hearthrug had kept it clean. They traced them with chalk that Robert had nicked from the top of the mathematical master's desk at school. You know, of course, that it is stealing to take a new stick of chalk, but it is not wrong to take a broken piece, so long as you only take one. (I do not know the reason of this rule, nor who made it.) And they chanted all the gloomiest songs they could think of. And, of course, nothing happened. So then Anthea said, "I'm sure a magic fire ought to be made of sweet-smelling wood, and have magic gums and essences and things in it."

"I don't know any sweet-smelling wood except cedar," said Robert, "but I've got some ends of cedar-wood lead pencil."

So they burned the ends of lead pencil. And still nothing happened.

"Let's burn some of the eucalyptus oil we have for our colds," said Anthea.

And they did. It certainly smelled very strong. And they

burned lumps of camphor out of the big chest. It was very
bright, and made a horrid black smoke, which looked very
magical. But still nothing happened. Then they got some
clean tea cloths from the dresser drawer in the kitchen, and
waved them over the magic chalk tracings, and sang "The
Hymn of the Moravian Nuns of Bethlehem," which is very
impressive. And still nothing happened. So they waved more
and more wildly, and Robert's tea cloth caught the golden
egg and whisked it off the mantelpiece, and it fell into the
fender and rolled under the grate.

"Oh, crikey!" said more than one voice.

And everyone instantly fell down flat on its front to look
under the grate, and there lay the egg, glowing in a nest of
hot ashes.

"It's not smashed, anyhow," said Robert, and he put his
hand under the grate and picked up the egg. But the egg was
much hotter than anyone would have believed it could
possibly get in such a short time, and Robert had to drop it
with a cry of "Bother!" It fell on the top bar of the grate and
bounced right into the glowing red-hot heart of the fire.

"The tongs!" cried Anthea. But alas, no one could remember where they were. Everyone had forgotten that the
tongs had last been used to fish up the doll's teapot from the
bottom of the water butt, where the Lamb had dropped it.
So the nursery tongs were resting between the water butt and
the dustbin, and Cook refused to lend the kitchen ones.

"Never mind," said Robert, "we'll get it out with the
poker and the shovel."

"Oh, stop," cried Anthea. "Look at it! Look! Look! Look!
I do believe something *is* going to happen!"

For the egg was now red hot, and inside it something was

moving. Next moment there was a soft cracking sound; the egg burst in two and out of it came a flame-colored bird. It rested a moment among the flames, and as it rested there the four children could see it growing bigger and bigger under their eyes.

The bird rose in its nest of fire, stretched its wings, and flew out into the room. It flew round and round, and round again, and where it passed the air was warm. Then it perched on the fender. The children looked at each other. Then Cyril put out a hand toward the bird. It put its head on one side and looked up at him, as you may have seen a parrot do when it is just going to speak, so that the children were hardly astonished at all when it said, "Be careful; I am not nearly cool yet."

They were not astonished, but they were very, very much interested.

They looked at the bird, and it was certainly worth looking at. Its feathers were like gold. It was about as large as a bantam, only its beak was not at all bantam-shaped.

"I believe I know what it is," said Robert. "I've seen a picture—"

He hurried away. A hasty dash and scramble among the papers on Father's study table yielded, as the sum books say, "the desired result." But when he came back into the room holding out a paper and crying "I say, look here," the others all said "Hush!" and he hushed obediently and instantly, for the bird was speaking.

"Which of you," it was saying, "put the egg into the fire?"

"He did," said three voices, and three fingers pointed at Robert.

The bird bowed; at least it was more like that than anything else.

"I am your grateful debtor," it said with a high-bred air.

The children were all choking with wonder and curiosity—
all except Robert. He held the paper in his hand, and he
*knew*. He said so. He said:

"*I* know who you are."

And he opened and displayed a printed paper, at the head
of which was a little picture of a bird sitting in a nest of
flames.

"You are the Phoenix," said Robert; and the bird was
quite pleased.

"My fame has lived then for two thousand years," it said.
"Allow me to look at my portrait."

It looked at the page which Robert, kneeling down, spread
out on the fender and said, "It's not a flattering likeness. . . .
And what are these characters?" it asked, pointing to the
printed part.

"Oh, that's all dullish; it's not much about *you*, you
know," said Cyril with unconscious politeness. "But you're
in lots of books—"

"With portraits?" asked the Phoenix.

"Well, no," said Cyril. "In fact, I don't think I ever saw
any portrait of you but that one, but I can read you something about yourself, if you like."

The Phoenix nodded, and Cyril went off and fetched
Volume X of the old encyclopedia, and on page 246 he
found the following:

"Phoenix—in ornithology, a fabulous bird of antiquity."

"Antiquity is quite correct," said the Phoenix, "but
fabulous—well, do I look it?"

Everyone shook its head.

Cyril went on: "The ancients speak of this bird as single, or the only one of its kind."

"That's right enough," said the Phoenix.

"They describe it as about the size of an eagle."

"Eagles are of different sizes," said the Phoenix. "It's not at all a good description."

All the children were kneeling on the hearthrug, to be as near the Phoenix as possible.

"You'll boil your brains," it said. "Look out, I'm nearly cool now." And with a whirr of golden wings it fluttered from the fender to the table. It was so nearly cool that there was only a very faint smell of burning when it had settled itself on the tablecloth.

"It's only a very little scorched," said the Phoenix, apologetically. "It will come out in the wash. Please go on reading."

The children gathered round the table.

"The size of an eagle," Cyril went on, "its head finely crested with a beautiful plumage, its neck covered with feathers of a gold color, and the rest of its body purple; only the tail white, and the eyes sparkling like stars. They say that it lives about five hundred years in the wilderness, and when advanced in age it builds itself a pile of sweet wood and aromatic gums, fires it with the wafting of its wings, and thus burns itself; and that from its ashes arises a worm, which in time grows up to be a Phoenix. Hence the Phoenicians gave—"

"Never mind what they gave," said the Phoenix, ruffling its golden feathers. "They never gave much, anyway; they always were people who gave nothing for nothing. That book ought to be destroyed. It's most inaccurate. The rest of my body was *never* purple, and as for my tail—well, I simply ask you, *is* it white?"

It turned round and gravely presented its golden tail to the children.

"No, it's not," said everybody.

"No, and it never was," said the Phoenix. "And that about the worm is just a vulgar insult. The Phoenix has an egg, like all respectable birds. It makes a pile—that part's all right—and it lays its egg, and it burns itself; and it goes to sleep and wakes up in its egg, and comes out and goes on living again, and so on forever and ever. I can't tell you how weary I got of it—such a restless existence; no repose."

"But how did your egg get *here*?" asked Anthea.

"Ah, that's my life secret," said the Phoenix. "I couldn't tell it to anyone who wasn't really sympathetic. I've always been a misunderstood bird. You can tell that by what they say about the worm. I might tell *you*," it went on, looking at Robert with eyes that were indeed starry. "*You* put me on the fire—"

Robert looked uncomfortable.

"The rest of us made the first of sweet-scented woods and gums, though," said Cyril.

"And—and it was an accident my putting you on the fire," said Robert, telling the truth with some difficulty, for he did not know how the Phoenix might take it. It took it in the most unexpected manner.

"Your candid avowal," it said, "removes my last scruple. I will tell you my story."

"And you won't vanish, or anything sudden, will you?" asked Anthea anxiously.

"Why?" it asked, puffing out the golden feathers. "Do you wish me to stay here?"

"Oh, *yes*," said everyone with unmistakable sincerity.

"Why?" asked the Phoenix again, looking modestly at the tablecloth.

"Because," said everyone at once, and then stopped short; only Jane added after a pause, "You are the most beautiful person we've ever seen."

"You are a sensible child," said the Phoenix, "and I will *not* vanish or anything sudden. And I will tell you my tale. I had resided, as your book says, for many thousand years in the wilderness, which is a large, quiet place with very little really good society, and I was becoming weary of the monotony of my existence. But I had acquired the habit of laying my egg and burning myself every five hundred years—and you know how difficult it is to break yourself of a habit."

"Yes," said Cyril. "Jane used to bite her nails."

"But I broke myself of it," urged Jane, rather hurt, "you know I did."

"Not till they put bitter aloes on them," said Cyril.

"I doubt," said the bird gravely, "whether even bitter aloes (the aloe, by the way, has a bad habit of its own, which it might well cure before seeking to cure others; I allude to its indolent practice of flowering but once a century), I doubt whether even bitter aloes could have cured *me*. But I *was* cured. I awoke one morning from a feverish dream—it was getting near the time for me to lay that tiresome fire and lay that tedious egg upon it—and I saw two people, a man and a woman. They were sitting on a carpet—and when I accosted them civilly they narrated to me their life story, which, as you have not yet heard it, I will now proceed to relate. They

were a prince and princess, and the story of their parents was
one which I am sure you will like to hear. In early youth the
mother of the princess happened to hear the story of a
certain enchanter, and in that story I am sure you will be
interested. The enchanter—"

"Oh, please, don't," said Anthea. "I can't understand all
these beginnings of stories, and you seem to be getting
deeper and deeper in them every minute. Do tell us your *own*
story. That's what we really want to hear."

"Well," said the Phoenix, seeming on the whole rather
flattered, "to cut about seventy long stories short (though *I*
had to listen to them all—but to be sure in the wilderness
there is plenty of time), this prince and princess were so fond
of each other that they did not want anyone else, and the
enchanter—don't be alarmed, I won't go into his history—
had given them a magic carpet (you've heard of a magic
carpet?), and they had just sat on it and told it to take them
right away from everyone—and it had brought them to the
wilderness. And as they meant to stay there they had no
further use for the carpet, so they gave it to me. That was
indeed the chance of a lifetime!"

"I don't see what you wanted with a carpet," said Jane,
"when you've got those lovely wings."

"They *are* nice wings, aren't they?" said the Phoenix,
simpering and spreading them out. "Well, I got the prince to
lay out the carpet, and I laid my egg on it; then I said to the
carpet, 'Now, my excellent carpet, prove your worth. Take
that egg somewhere where it can't be hatched for two thousand years, and where, when that time's up, someone will
light a fire of sweet wood and aromatic gums, and put the
egg in to hatch'; and you see it's all come out exactly as I

said. The words were no sooner out of my beak than egg and carpet disappeared. The royal lovers assisted to arrange my pile, and soothed my last moments. I burnt myself up, and knew no more till I awoke on yonder altar."

It pointed its claw at the grate.

"But the carpet," said Robert, "the magic carpet that takes you anywhere you wish. What became of that?"

"Oh, *that?*" said the Phoenix carelessly. "I should say that that *is* the carpet. I remember the pattern perfectly."

It pointed as it spoke to the floor, where lay the carpet which Mother had bought in the Kentish Town Road for twenty-two shillings and ninepence.

At that instant Father's latchkey was heard in the door.

"Oh," whispered Cyril, "now we shall catch it for not being in bed."

"Wish yourself there," said the Phoenix in a hurried whisper, "and then wish the carpet back in its place."

No sooner said than done. It made one a little giddy, certainly, and a little breathless; but when things seemed right way up again, there the children were, in bed, and the lights were out.

They heard the soft voice of the Phoenix through the darkness.

"I shall sleep on the cornice above your curtains," it said. "Please don't mention me to your kinsfolk."

"Not much good," said Robert. "They'd never believe us. I say," he called through the half-open door to the girls, "talk about adventures and things happening. We ought to be able to get some fun out of a magic carpet *and* a Phoenix."

"Rather," said the girls, from bed.

"Children," said Father, on the stairs, "go to sleep at once. What do you mean by talking at this time of night?"

No answer was expected to this question, but under the bedclothes Cyril murmured one.

"Mean?" he said. "Don't know what we mean. I don't know what *anything* means—"

"But we've got a magic carpet *and* a Phoenix," said Robert.

"You'll get something else if Father comes in and catches you," said Cyril. "Shut up, I tell you."

Robert shut up. But he knew as well as you do that the adventures of that carpet and that Phoenix were only just beginning.

Father and Mother had not the least idea of what had happened in their absence. This is often the case, even when there are no magic carpets or Phoenixes in the house.

The next morning—but I am sure you would rather wait till the next chapter before you hear about *that*.

# Chapter 2

# The Topless Tower

*T*he children had seen the Phoenix egg hatched in the flames in their own nursery grate, and had heard from it how the carpet on their own nursery floor was really the wishing carpet, which would take them anywhere they chose. The carpet had transported them to bed just at the right moment, and the Phoenix had gone to roost on the cornice supporting the window curtains of the boys' room.

"Excuse me," said a gentle voice, and a courteous beak opened, very kindly and delicately, the right eye of Cyril. "I hear the slaves below preparing food. Awaken! A word of explanation and arrangement . . . I do wish you wouldn't—"

The Phoenix stopped speaking and fluttered away crossly to the cornice pole; for Cyril had hit out, as boys will do when they are awakened suddenly, and the Phoenix was not used to boys, and his feelings, if not his wings, were hurt.

"Sorry," said Cyril, coming awake all in a minute. "Do come back! What was it you were saying? Something about bacon and rations?"

The Phoenix fluttered back to the brass rail at the foot of the bed.

"I say—you *are* real," said Cyril. "How ripping! And the carpet?"

"The carpet is as real as it ever was," said the Phoenix rather contemptuously. "But, of course, a carpet's only a carpet, whereas a Phoenix is superlatively a Phoenix."

"Yes, indeed," said Cyril, "I see it is. Oh, what luck! Wake up, Bobs! There's jolly well something to wake up for today. And it's Saturday too."

"I've been reflecting," said the Phoenix, "during the silent watches of the night, and I could not avoid the conclusion that you were quite insufficiently astonished at my appearance yesterday. The ancients were always *very* surprised. Did you, by chance, *expect* my egg to hatch?"

"Not us," Cyril said.

"And if we had," said Anthea, who had come in in her nightie when she heard the silvery voice of the Phoenix, "we could never, never have expected it to hatch anything so splendid as you."

The bird smiled. Perhaps you've never seen a bird smile?

"You see," said Anthea, wrapping herself in the boys' counterpane, for the morning was chill, "we've had things happen to us before"; and she told the story of the Psammead, or sand fairy.

"Ah, yes," said the Phoenix. "Psammeads were rare, even in my time. I remember I used to be called the Psammead of the Desert. I was always having compliments paid me; I can't think why."

"Can *you* give wishes, then?" asked Jane, who had now come in too.

"Oh, dear me, no," said the Phoenix contemptuously, "at least—but I hear footsteps approaching. I hasten to conceal myself." And it did.

I think I said that this day was Saturday. It was also Cook's birthday, and Mother had allowed her and Eliza to go to the Crystal Palace with a party of friends, so Jane and Anthea of course had to help to make beds and to wash up the breakfast cups, and little things like that. Robert and Cyril intended to spend the morning in conversation with the Phoenix, but the bird had its own ideas about this.

"I must have an hour or two's quiet," it said, "I really must. My nerves will give way unless I can get a little rest. You must remember it's two thousand years since I had any conversation—I'm out of practice, and I must take care of myself. I've often been told that mine is a valuable life." So it nestled down inside an old hat box of Father's, which had been brought down from the box room some days before, when a helmet was suddenly needed for a game of tournaments, with its golden head under its golden wing, and went to sleep. So then Robert and Cyril moved the table back, and were going to sit on the carpet and wish themselves somewhere else. But before they could decide on the place, Cyril said:

"I don't know. Perhaps it's rather sneakish to begin without the girls."

"They'll be all the morning," said Robert impatiently. And then a thing inside him, which tiresome books sometimes call the "inward monitor," said, "Why don't you help them, then?"

Cyril's "inward monitor" happened to say the same thing at the same moment, so the boys went and helped to wash

up the tea cups, and to dust the drawing room. Robert was so
interested that he proposed to clean the front doorsteps—a
thing he had never been allowed to do. Nor was he allowed
to do it on this occasion. One reason was that it had already
been done by Cook.

When all the housework was finished, the girls dressed the
happy, wriggling baby in his blue highwayman coat and
three-cornered hat, and kept him amused while Mother
changed her dress and got ready to take him over to Granny's. Mother always went to Granny's every Saturday, and
generally some of the children went with her; but today they
were to keep house. And their hearts were full of joyous and
delightful feelings every time they remembered that the house
they would have to keep had a Phoenix in it, *and* a wishing
carpet.

You can always keep the Lamb good and happy for quite a
long time if you play the Noah's Ark game with him. It is
quite simple. He just sits on your lap and tells you what
animal he is, and then you say the little poetry piece about
whatever animal he chooses to be. Of course, some of the
animals, like the zebra and the tiger, haven't got any poetry,
because they are so difficult to rhyme to. The Lamb knows
quite well which are the poetry animals.

"I'm a baby bear!" said the Lamb, snugging down; and
Anthea began:

> "I love my little baby bear,
> I love his nose and toes and hair;
> I like to hold him in my arm,
> And keep him *very* safe and warm."

And when she said "very," of course there was a real bear's hug.

Then came the eel, and the Lamb was tickled till he wriggled exactly like a real one:

> "I love my little baby eel,
> He is so squidglety to feel;
> He'll be an eel when he is big—
> But now he's just—a—tiny *snig*!"

Perhaps you didn't know that a snig was a baby eel? It is, though, and the Lamb knew it.

"Hedgehog now!" he said; and Anthea went on:

> "My baby hedgehog, how I like ye,
> Though your back's so prickly spiky;
> Your front is very soft, I've found,
> So I must love you front ways round."

And then she loved him front ways round, while he squealed with pleasure.

It is a very baby game, and, of course, the rhymes are only meant for very, very small people—not for people who are old enough to read books, so I won't tell you any more of them.

By the time the Lamb had been a baby lion and a baby weasel, and a baby rabbit and a baby rat, Mother was ready; and she and the Lamb, having been kissed by everybody and hugged as thoroughly as it is possible to be when you're dressed for out of doors, were seen to the tram by the boys. When the boys came back, everyone looked at every one else and said:

"Now!"

They locked the front door and they locked the back door, and they fastened all the windows. They moved the table and chairs off the carpet, and Anthea swept it.

"We must show it a *little* attention," she said kindly. "We'll give it tea leaves next time. Carpets like tea leaves."

Then everyone put on its outdoor things, because, as Cyril said, they didn't know where they might be going, and it makes people stare if you go out of doors in November in pinafores and without hats.

Then Robert gently awoke the Phoenix, who yawned and stretched itself, and allowed Robert to lift it on the middle of the carpet, where it instantly went to sleep again with its crested head tucked under its golden wing as before. Then everyone sat down on the carpet.

"Where shall we go?" was of course the question, and it was warmly discussed. Anthea wanted to go to Japan. Robert and Cyril voted for America, and Jane wished to go to the seaside.

"Because there are donkeys there," said she.

"Not in November, silly," said Cyril; and the discussion got warmer and warmer, and still nothing was settled.

"I vote we let the Phoenix decide," said Robert at last. So they stroked it till it woke.

"We want to go somewhere abroad," they said, "and we can't make up our minds where."

"Let the carpet make up *its* mind, if it has one," said the Phoenix. "Just say you wish to go abroad."

So they did; and the next moment the world seemed to spin upside down, and when it was right way up again and they were ungiddy enough to look about them, they were out of doors.

Out of doors—that is a feeble way to express where they were. They were out of—out of the earth, or off it. In fact, they were floating steadily, safely, splendidly, in the crisp clear air, with the pale bright blue of the sky above them, and far down below the pale bright sun-diamonded waves of the sea. The carpet had stiffened itself somehow, so that it was square and firm like a raft, and it steered itself so beautifully and kept on its way so flat and fearless that no one was at all afraid of tumbling off. In front of them lay land.

"The coast of France," said the Phoenix, waking up and pointing with its wing. "Where do you wish to go? I should always keep *one* wish, of course—for emergencies—otherwise you may get into an emergency from which you can't emerge at all."

But the children were far too deeply interested to listen.

"I tell you what," said Cyril. "Let's let the thing go on and on, and when we see a place we really want to stop at—why, we'll just stop. Isn't this ripping?"

"It's like trains," said Anthea, as they swept over the low-lying coastline and held a steady course above orderly fields and straight roads bordered with poplar trees. "Like express trains, only in trains you never can see anything because of grown-ups wanting the windows shut; and then they breathe on them, and it's like ground glass, and nobody can see anything, and then they go to sleep."

"It's like tobogganing," said Robert, "so fast and smooth, only there's no doormat to stop short on—it goes on and on."

"You darling Phoenix," said Jane, "it's all your doing. Oh, look at that ducky little church and the women with flappy cappy things on their heads."

"Don't mention it," said the Phoenix with sleepy politeness.

"*Oh!*" said Cyril, summing up all the rapture that was in every heart. "Look at it all—look at it—and think of the Kentish Town Road."

Everyone looked and everyone thought. And the glorious, gliding, smooth, steady rush went on, and they looked down on strange and beautiful things, and held their breath and let it go in deep sighs, and said "Oh!" and "Ah!" till it was long past dinnertime.

It was Jane who suddenly said, "If only we'd brought that jam tart and cold mutton with us. It would have been jolly to have a picnic in the air."

The jam tart and cold mutton were, however, far away, sitting quietly in the larder of the house in Camden Town which the children were supposed to be keeping. A mouse was at that moment tasting the outside of the raspberry jam part of the tart (she had nibbled a sort of gulf, or bay, through the pastry edge) to see whether it was the sort of dinner she could ask her little mouse husband to sit down to. She had had a very good dinner herself. It is an ill wind that blows nobody any good.

"We'll stop as soon as we see a nice place," said Anthea. "I've got threepence, and you boys have the fourpence each that your trams didn't cost the other day, so we can buy things to eat. I expect the Phoenix can speak French."

The carpet was sailing along over rocks and rivers and trees and towns and farms and fields. It reminded everybody of a certain time when all of them had had wings, and had flown up to the top of a church tower, and had had a feast there of chicken and tongue and new bread and soda water. And this again reminded them how hungry they were. And just as they were all being reminded of this very strongly indeed, they saw ahead of them some ruined walls on a hill, and strong and upright, and really, to look at, as good as new—a great square tower.

"The top of that's just the exactly same size as the carpet," said Jane. "I think it would be good to go to the top of that, because then none of the Abby-what's-its-names—I mean natives—would be able to take the carpet away even if they wanted to. And some of us could go out and get things to eat—buy them honestly, I mean, not take them out of larder windows."

"I think it would be better if we went—" Anthea was beginning; but Jane suddenly clenched her hands.

"I don't see why I should never do anything I want, just because I'm the youngest. I wish the carpet would fit itself in at the top of that tower—so there!"

The carpet made a disconcerting bound, and next moment it was hovering above the square top of the tower. Then slowly and carefully it began to sink under them. It was like a lift going down with you at the Army and Navy Stores.

"I don't think we ought to wish things without all agreeing to them first," said Robert huffishly. "Hullo! What on earth?"

For unexpectedly and grayly something was coming up all round the four sides of the carpet. It was as if a wall were being built by magic quickness. It was a foot high—it was two feet high—three, four, five. It was shutting out the light—more and more.

Anthea looked up at the sky and the walls that now rose six feet above them.

"We're dropping into the tower," she screamed. "*There wasn't any top to it.* So the carpet's going to fit itself in at the bottom."

Robert sprang to his feet.

"We ought to have— Hullo! an owl's nest." He put his knee on a jutting smooth piece of gray stone, and reached his hand into a deep window slit—broad to the inside of the tower and narrowing like a funnel to the outside.

"Look sharp!" cried everyone, but Robert did not look sharp enough. By the time he had drawn his hand out of the owl's nest—there were no eggs there—the carpet had sunk eight feet below him.

"Jump, you silly cuckoo!" cried Cyril with brotherly anxiety.

But Robert couldn't turn round all in a minute into a jumping position. He wriggled and twisted and got on to the broad ledge, and by the time he was ready to jump the walls of the tower had risen up thirty feet above the others, who were still sinking with the carpet, and Robert found himself in the embrasure of a window; alone, for even the owls were not at home that day. The wall was smoothish; there was no climbing up, and as for climbing down—Robert hid his face in his hands and squirmed back and back from the giddy verge, until the back part of him was wedged quite tight in the narrowest part of the window slit.

He was safe now, of course, but the outside part of his window was like a frame to a picture of part of the other side of the tower. It was very pretty, with moss growing between the stones and little shiny gems; but between him and it there was the width of the tower, and nothing in it but

empty air. The situation was terrible. Robert saw in a flash
that the carpet was likely to bring them into just the same
sort of tight places that they used to get into with the wishes
the Psammead granted them.

And the others—imagine their feelings as the carpet sank
slowly and steadily to the very bottom of the tower, leaving
Robert clinging to the wall. Robert did not even try to
imagine their feelings—he had quite enough to do with his
own; but you can.

As soon as the carpet came to a stop on the ground at the
bottom of the inside of the tower it suddenly lost that raftlike
stiffness which had been such a comfort during the journey
from Camden Town to the topless tower, and spread itself
limply over the loose stones and little earthy mounds at the
bottom of the tower, just exactly like any ordinary carpet.
Also it shrank suddenly, so that it seemed to draw away from
under their feet, and they stepped quickly off the edges and
stood on the firm ground, while the carpet drew itself in till
it was its proper size, and no longer fitted exactly into the
inside of the tower, but left quite a big space all round it.

Then across the carpet they looked at each other, and
then every chin was tilted up and every eye sought vainly to
see where poor Robert had got to. Of course, they couldn't
see him.

"If only we hadn't come," said Jane.

"Look here, we can't leave Robert up there," said Cyril. "I
wish the carpet would fetch him down."

The carpet seemed to awake from a dream and pull itself
together. It stiffened itself briskly and floated up between the
four walls of the tower. The children below craned their
heads back and nearly broke their necks in doing it. The

carpet rose and rose. It hung poised darkly above them for an anxious moment or two; then it dropped down again, threw itself on the uneven floor of the tower, and as it did so it tumbled Robert out of the uneven floor of the tower.

"Oh, glory!" said Robert, "that was a squeak. You don't know how I felt. I say, I've had about enough for a bit. Let's wish ourselves at home again and have a go at that jam tart and mutton. We can go out again afterward."

"Righto!" said everyone, for the adventure had shaken the nerves of all. So they all got on to the carpet again, and said:

"I wish we were at home."

And lo and behold, they were no more at home than before. The carpet never moved. The Phoenix had taken the opportunity to go to sleep. Anthea woke it up gently.

"Look here," she said.

"I'm looking," said the Phoenix.

"We wished to be at home, and we're still here," complained Jane.

"No," said the Phoenix, looking about it at the high dark walls of the tower. "No; I quite see that."

"But we *wished* to be at home," said Cyril.

"No doubt," said the bird politely.

"And the carpet hasn't moved an inch," said Robert.

"No," said the Phoenix, "I see it hasn't."

"But I thought it was a wishing carpet?"

"So it is," said the Phoenix.

"Then why—?" asked the children, all together.

"I did tell you, you know," said the Phoenix, "only you are so fond of listening to the music of your own voices. It is, indeed, the most lovely music to each of us, and therefore—"

"You did tell us *what?*" interrupted an exasperated Robert.

"Why, that the carpet only gives you three wishes a day and *you've had them.*"

There was a heartfelt silence.

"Then how are we going to get home?" said Cyril, at last.

"I haven't any idea," replied the Phoenix kindly. "Can I fly out and get you any little thing?"

"How could you carry the money to pay for it?"

"It isn't necessary. Birds always take what they want. It is not regarded as stealing, except in the case of magpies."

The children were glad to find they had been right in supposing this to be the case, on the day when they had had wings, and enjoyed somebody else's ripe plums.

"Yes; let the Phoenix get us something to eat, anyway," Robert urged. ("If it will be so kind, you mean," corrected Anthea in a whisper.) "If it will be so kind, and we can be thinking while it's gone."

So the Phoenix fluttered up through the gray space of the tower and vanished at the top, and it was not till it had quite gone that Jane said:

"Suppose it never comes back."

It was not a pleasant thought, and though Anthea at once said, "Of course it will come back; I'm certain it's a bird of its word," a further gloom was cast by the idea. For, curiously enough, there was no door to the tower, and all the windows were far, far too high to be reached by the most adventurous climber. It was cold, too, and Anthea shivered.

"Yes," said Cyril, "it's like being at the bottom of a well."

The children waited in a sad and hungry silence, and got little stiff necks with holding their little heads back to look up the inside of the tall gray tower, to see if the Phoenix were coming.

At last it came. It looked very big as it fluttered down between the walls, and as it neared them the children saw that its bigness was caused by a basket of boiled chestnuts which it carried in one claw. In the other hand it held a piece of bread. And in its beak was a very large pear. The pear was juicy, and as good as a very small drink. When the meal was over everyone felt better, and the question of how to get home was discussed without any disagreeableness. But no one could think of any way out of the difficulty, or even out of the tower; for the Phoenix, though its beak and claws had fortunately been strong enough to carry food for them, was plainly not equal to flying through the air with four well-nourished children.

"We must stay here, I suppose," said Robert at last, "and shout out every now and then, and someone will hear us and bring ropes and ladders, and rescue us like out of mines; and they'll get up a subscription to send us home, like castaways."

"Yes; but we shan't be home before Mother is, and then Father'll take away the carpet and say it's dangerous or something," said Cyril.

"I *do* wish we hadn't come," said Jane.

And everyone else said "Shut up," except Anthea, who suddenly awoke the Phoenix and said:

"Look here, I believe *you* can help us. Oh, I do wish you would!"

"I will help you as far as lies in my power," said the Phoenix at once. "What is it you want now?"

"Why, we want to get home," said everyone.

"Oh," said the Phoenix. "Ah, hum! Yes. Home, you said? Meaning?"

"Where we live—where we slept last night—where the altar is that your egg was hatched on."

"Oh, there!" said the Phoenix. "Well, I'll do my best." It fluttered on to the carpet and walked up and down for a few minutes in deep thought. Then it drew itself up proudly.

"I *can* help you," it said. "I am almost sure I can help you. Unless I am grossly deceived I can help you. You won't mind my leaving you for an hour or two?" And without waiting for a reply it soared up through the dimness of the tower into the brightness above.

"Now," said Cyril firmly, "it said an hour or two. But I've read about captives and people shut up in dungeons and catacombs and things awaiting release, and I know each moment is an eternity. Those people always do something to pass the desperate moments. It's no use our trying to tame spiders, because we shan't have time."

"I *hope* not," said Jane doubtfully.

"But we ought to scratch our names on the stones or something."

"I say, talking of stones," said Robert, "you see that heap of stones against the wall over in that corner? Well, I'm certain there's a hole in the wall there—and I believe it's a door. Yes, look here—the stones are round like an arch in the wall, and here's the hole—it's all black inside."

He had walked over to the heap as he spoke and climbed up to it—dislodged the top stone of the heap and uncovered a little dark space.

Next moment everyone was helping to pull down the heap of stones, and very soon everyone threw off its jacket, for it was warm work.

"It *is* a door," said Cyril, wiping his face, "and not a bad thing either, if—"

He was going to add, "if anything happens to the Phoenix," but he didn't, for fear of frightening Jane. He was not an unkind boy when he had leisure to think of such things.

The arched hole in the wall grew larger and larger. It was very, very black, even compared with the sort of twilight at the bottom of the tower; it grew larger because the children kept pulling off the stones and throwing them down into another heap. The stones must have been there a very long time, for they were covered with moss, and some of them were stuck together by it. So it was fairly hard work, as Robert pointed out.

When the hole reached to about halfway between the top of the arch and the tower, Robert and Cyril let themselves down cautiously on the inside, and lit matches. How thankful they felt then that they had a sensible father, who did not forbid them to carry matches, as some boys' fathers do. The father of Robert and Cyril only insisted on the matches being of the kind that strike only on the box.

"It's not a door, it's a sort of tunnel," Robert cried to the girls, after the first match had flared up, flickered, and gone out. "Stand off—we'll push some more stones down!"

They did, amid deep excitement. And now the stone heap was almost gone—and before them the girls saw the dark archway leading to unknown things. All doubts and fears as to getting home were forgotten in this thrilling moment. It was like Monte Cristo—it was like—

"I say," cried Anthea suddenly, "come out! There's always bad air in places that have been shut up. It makes your

torches go out, and then you die. It's called fire damp, I
believe. Come out, I tell you."

The urgency of her tone actually brought the boys out—
and then everyone took up its jacket and fanned the dark
arch with it, so as to make the air fresh inside. When Anthea
thought the air inside "must be freshened by now," Cyril led
the way into the arch. The girls followed, and Robert came
last, because Jane refused to tail the procession lest "something" should come in after her and catch her from behind.
Cyril advanced cautiously, lighting match after match and
peering before him.

"It's a vaulting roof," he said, "and it's all stone—all right,
Panther, don't keep pulling at my jacket! The air must be all
right because of the matches, silly, and there are—look
out—there are steps down."

"Oh, don't let's go any farther," said Jane, in an agony of
reluctance (a very painful thing, by the way, to be in). "I'm
sure there are snakes, or dens of lions, or something. Do let's
go back, and come some other time, with candles, and
bellows for the fire damp."

"Let me get in front of you, then," said the stern voice of
Robert, from behind. "This is exactly the place for buried
treasure, and I'm going on, anyway; you can stay behind if
you like." And then, of course, Jane consented to go on.

So, very slowly and carefully, the children went down the
steps—there were seventeen of them—and at the bottom of
the steps were more passages branching four ways, and a sort
of low arch on the right hand side made Cyril wonder what
it could be, for it was too low to be the beginning of another
passage.

So he knelt down and lit a match and, stooping very low, he peeped in.

"There's *something*," he said, and reached out his hand. It touched something that felt more like a damp bag of marbles than anything else that Cyril had ever touched.

"I believe it *is* a buried treasure," he cried.

And it was; for even as Anthea cried, "Oh, hurry up, Squirrel—fetch it out!" Cyril pulled out a rotting canvas bag—about as big as the paper ones the greengrocer gives you with Barcelona nuts* in for sixpence.

"There's more of it, a lot more," he said.

As he pulled, the rotten bag gave way, and the gold coins ran and spun and jumped and bumped and chinked and clinked on the floor of the dark passage.

I wonder what you would say if you suddenly came upon a buried treasure? What Cyril said was, "Oh, bother—I've burnt my fingers!" and as he spoke he dropped the match. "*And it was the last!*" he added.

There was a moment of desperate silence. Then Jane began to cry.

"Don't," said Anthea, "don't, Pussy—you'll exhaust the air if you cry. We can get out all right."

"Yes," said Jane, through her sobs, "and find the Phoenix has come back and gone away again—because it thought we'd gone home some other way, and—Oh, I *wish* we hadn't come."

Everyone stood quite still—only Anthea cuddled Jane up to her and tried to wipe her eyes in the dark.

---

*Hazelnuts

"*D—don't*," said Jane. "That's my *ear*—I'm not crying with my ears."

"Come, let's get on out," said Robert; but that was not so easy, for no one could remember exactly which way they had come. It is very difficult to remember things in the dark, unless you have matches with you, and then of course it is quite different, even if you don't strike one.

Everyone had come to agree with Jane's constant wish— and despair was making the darkness blacker than ever— when quite suddenly the floor seemed to tip up—and a strong sensation of being in a whirling lift came upon everyone. All eyes were closed—one's eyes always are in the dark, don't you think? When the whirling feeling stopped, Cyril said, "Earthquakes!" and they all opened their eyes.

They were in their own dingy breakfast room at home, and oh, how light and bright and safe and pleasant and altogether delightful it seemed after that dark underground tunnel! The carpet lay on the floor, looking as calm as though it had never been for an excursion in its life. On the mantelpiece stood the Phoenix, waiting with an air of modest yet sterling worth for the thanks of the children.

"But how *did* you do it?" they asked, when everyone had thanked the Phoenix again and again.

"Oh, I just went and got a wish from your friend the Psammead."

"But how *did* you know where to find it?"

"I found that out from the carpet; these wishing creatures always know all about each other—they're so clannish; like the Scots, you know—all related."

"But the carpet can't talk, can it?"

"No."

"Then how—"

"How did I get the Psammead's address? I tell you I got it from the carpet."

"*Did* it speak, then?"

"No," said the Phoenix thoughtfully, "it didn't speak, but I gathered my information from something in its manner. I was always a singularly observant bird."

It was not till after the cold mutton and the jam tart, as well as the tea and bread and butter, that anyone found time to regret the golden treasure which had been left scattered on the floor of the underground passage, and which, indeed, no one had thought of till now, since the moment when Cyril burnt his fingers at the flame of the last match.

"What owls and goats we were!" said Robert. "Look how we've always wanted treasure. And now—"

"Never mind," said Anthea, trying as usual to make the best of it. "We'll go back again and get it all, and then we'll give everybody presents."

More than a quarter of an hour passed most agreeably in arranging what presents should be given to whom, and, when the claims of generosity had been satisfied, the talk ran for fifty minutes on what they would buy for themselves.

It was Cyril who broke in on Robert's almost too technical account of the motor car in which he meant to go to and from school.

"There!" he said. "Dry up. It's no good. We can't ever go back. We don't know where it is."

"Don't *you* know?" Jane asked the Phoenix wistfully.

"Not in the least," the Phoenix replied in a tone of amiable regret.

"Then we've lost the treasure," said Cyril.

And they had.

"But we've got the carpet and the Phoenix," said Anthea.

"Excuse me," said the bird with an air of wounded dignity, "I do *so hate* to seem to interfere, but surely you *must* mean the Phoenix and the carpet?"

# Chapter 3

# The Queen Cook

*I*t was on a Saturday that the children made their first glorious journey on the wishing carpet. Unless you are too young to read at all, you will know that the next day must have been Sunday.

Sunday at 18, Camden Terrace, Camden Town, was always a very pretty day. Father always brought home flowers on Saturday, so that the breakfast table was extra beautiful. In November, of course, the flowers were chrysanthemums, yellow and coppery colored. Then there were always sausages on toast for breakfast, and these are rapture, after six days of Kentish Town Road eggs at fourteen a shilling.

On this particular Sunday there were fowls for dinner, a kind of food that is generally kept for birthdays and grand occasions, and there was an angel pudding, when rice and milk and oranges and white icing do their best to make you happy.

After dinner Father was very sleepy indeed, because he had been working hard all the week; but he did not yield to the voice that said "Go and have an hour's rest." He nursed

the Lamb, who had a horrid cough that Cook said was
whooping cough as sure as eggs, and he said:

"Come along, kiddies; I've got a ripping book from the
library, called *The Golden Age*, and I'll read it to you."

Mother settled herself on the drawing-room sofa, and said
she could listen quite nicely with her eyes shut. The Lamb
snugged into the "armchair corner" of Daddy's arm, and the
others got into a happy heap on the hearthrug. At first, of
course, there were too many feet and knees and shoulders
and elbows, but real comfort was actually settling down on
them, and the Phoenix and the carpet were put away on the
back top shelf of their minds (beautiful things that could be
taken out and played with later), when a surly solid knock
came at the drawing-room door. It opened an angry inch,
and the cook's voice said, "Please, ma'am, may I speak to
you a moment!"

Mother looked at Father with a desperate expression. Then
she put her pretty sparkly Sunday shoes down from the sofa,
and stood up in them and sighed.

"As good fish in the sea," said Father cheerfully, and it
was not till much later that the children understood what he
meant.

Mother went out into the passage, which is called "the
hall," where the umbrella stand is, and the picture of the
Monarch of the Glen in a yellow shining frame, with brown
spots on the Monarch from the damp in the house before
last, and there was Cook, very red and damp in the face, and
with clean apron tied on all crooked over the dirty one that
she had dished up those dear delightful chickens in. She
stood there and she seemed to get redder and damper, and

she twisted the corner of her apron round her fingers, and
she said very shortly and fiercely:

"If you please, ma'am, I should wish to leave at my day
month."

Mother leaned against the hatstand. The children could
see her looking pale through the crack of the door, because
she had been very kind to the cook, and had given her a
holiday only the day before, and it seemed so very unkind of
the cook to want to go like this, and on a Sunday too.

"Why, what's the matter?" Mother said.

"It's them children," the cook replied, and somehow the
children all felt that they had known it from the first. They
did not remember having done anything extra wrong, but it is
so frightfully easy to displease a cook. "It's them children:
there's that there new carpet in their room, covered thick
with mud, both sides, beastly yellow mud, and sakes alive
knows where they got it. And all that muck to clean up on a
Sunday! It's not my place, and it's not my intentions, so I
don't deceive you, ma'am, and but for them limbs, which
they is if ever there was, it's not a bad place, though I says it,
and I wouldn't wish to leave, but—"

"I'm very sorry," said Mother gently. "I will speak to the
children. And you had better think it over, and if you *really*
wish to go, tell me tomorrow!"

Next day Mother had a quiet talk with Cook, and Cook
said she didn't mind if she stayed on a bit, just to see.

But meantime the question of the muddy carpet had been
gone into thoroughly by Father and Mother. Jane's candid
explanation that the mud had come from the bottom of a
foreign tower where there was buried treasure was received
with such chilling disbelief that the others limited their

defense to an expression of sorrow, and of a determination "not to do it again." But Father said (and Mother agreed with him, because mothers have to agree with fathers, and not because it was her own idea) that children who coated a carpet on both sides with thick mud, and when they were asked for an explanation could only talk silly nonsense—that meant Jane's truthful statement—were not fit to have a carpet at all and, indeed, *shouldn't* have one for a week!

So the carpet was brushed (with tea leaves, too, which was the only comfort Anthea could think of) and folded up and put away in the cupboard at the top of the stairs, and Daddy put the key in his trousers pocket.

"Till Saturday," said he.

"Never mind," said Anthea, "we've got the Phoenix."

But, as it happened, they hadn't. The Phoenix was nowhere to be found, and everything had suddenly settled down from the rosy wild beauty of magic happenings to the common damp brownness of ordinary November life in Camden Town—and there was the nursery floor all bare boards in the middle and brown oilcloth round the outside, and the bareness and yellowness of the middle floor showed up the blackbeetles with terrible distinctness, when the poor things came out in the evening, as usual, to try to make friends with the children. But the children never would.

The Sunday ended in gloom, which even junket for supper in the blue Dresden bowl could hardly lighten at all. Next day the Lamb's cough was worse. It certainly seemed very whoopy, and the doctor came in his brougham carriage.

Everyone tried to bear up under the weight of the sorrow which it was to know that the wishing carpet was locked up and the Phoenix mislaid. A good deal of time was spent in looking for the Phoenix.

"It's a bird of its word," said Anthea. "I'm sure it's not deserted us. But you know it had a most awfully long fly from wherever it was to near Rochester and back, and I expect the poor thing's feeling tired out and wants rest. I am sure we may trust it."

The others tried to feel sure of this too, but it was hard.

No one could be expected to feel very kindly toward the cook, since it was entirely through her making such a fuss about a little foreign mud that the carpet had been taken away.

"She might have told 'us," said Jane, "and Panther and I would have cleaned it with tea leaves."

"She's a cantankerous cat," said Robert.

"I shan't say what I think about her," said Anthea primly, "because it would be evil speaking, lying, and slandering."

"It's not lying to say she's a disagreeable pig, and a beastly blue-nosed Bozwoz," said Cyril, who had read *The Eyes of Light* and intended to talk like Tony as soon as he could teach Robert to talk like Paul.

And all the children, even Anthea, agreed that even if she wasn't a blue-nosed Bozwoz, they wished Cook had never been born.

But I ask you to believe that they didn't do all the things on purpose which so annoyed the cook during the following week, though I daresay the things would not have happened if the cook had been a favorite.

This is a mystery. Explain it if you can.

The things that had happened were as follows:

*Sunday.* Discovery of foreign mud on both sides of the carpet.

*Monday.* Licorice put on to boil with aniseed balls in a saucepan. Anthea did this, because she thought it would be good for the Lamb's cough. The whole thing forgotten, and bottom of saucepan burned out. It was the little saucepan lined with white that was kept for the baby's milk.

*Tuesday.* A dead mouse found in pantry. Fish slice taken to dig grave with. By regrettable accident fish slice broken. Defense: "The cook oughtn't to keep dead mice in pantries."

*Wednesday.* Chopped suet left on kitchen table. Robert added chopped soap, but he says he thought the suet was soap too.

*Thursday.* Broke the kitchen window by falling against it during a perfectly fair game of bandits in the area.

*Friday.* Stopped up grating of kitchen sink with putty and filled sink with water to make a lake to sail paper boats in. Went away and left the tap running. Kitchen hearthrug and Cook's shoes ruined.

On Saturday the carpet was restored. There had been plenty of time during the week to decide where it should be asked to go when they did get back.

Mother had gone over to Granny's and had taken the Lamb because he had a bad cough, which, Cook repeated, was whooping cough as sure as eggs is eggs.

"But we'll take him out, a ducky darling," said Anthea. "We'll take him somewhere where you can't have whooping cough. Don't be so silly, Robert. If he *does* talk about it no one'll take any notice. He's always talking about the things he's never seen."

So they dressed the Lamb and themselves in out-of-door

clothes, and the Lamb chuckled and coughed, and laughed and coughed again, poor dear, and all the chairs and tables were moved off the carpet by the boys, while Jane nursed the Lamb, and Anthea rushed through the house in one last wild hunt for the missing Phoenix.

"It's no use waiting for it," she said, reappearing breathless in the breakfast room. "But I know it hasn't deserted us. It's a bird of its word."

"Quite so," said the gentle voice of the Phoenix from beneath the table.

Everyone fell on its knees and looked up, and there was the Phoenix perched on a crossbar of wood that ran across under the table, and had once supported a drawer, in the happy days before the drawer had been used as a boat, and its bottom unfortunately trodden out by Raggett's Really Reliable School Boots on the feet of Robert.

"I've been here all the time," said the Phoenix, yawning politely behind its claw. "If you wanted me you should have recited the ode of invocation; it's seven thousand lines long, and written in very pure and beautiful Greek."

"Couldn't you tell it us in English?" asked Anthea.

"It's rather long, isn't it?" said Jane, jumping the Lamb on her knee.

"Couldn't you make a short English version, like Tate and Brady?"

"Oh, come along, do," said Robert, holding out his hand. "Come along, good old Phoenix."

"Good old *beautiful* Phoenix," it corrected shyly.

"Good old *beautiful* Phoenix, then. Come along, come along," said Robert impatiently, with his hand still held out.

The Phoenix fluttered at once on to his wrist.

"This amiable youth," it said to the others, "has miraculously been able to put the whole meaning of the seven thousand lines of Greek invocation into one English hexameter. A little misplaced some of the words, but—"

"Oh, come along, come along, good old beautiful Phoenix."

"Not perfect, I admit—but not bad for a boy of his age."

"Well, *now* then," said Robert, stepping back on to the carpet with the golden Phoenix on his wrist.

"You look like the king's falconer," said Jane, sitting down on the carpet with the baby on her lap.

Robert tried to go on looking like it. Cyril and Anthea stood on the carpet.

"We shall have to get back before dinner," said Cyril, "or Cook will blow the gaff."

"She hasn't sneaked since Sunday," said Anthea.

"She—" Robert was beginning, when the door burst open and the cook, fierce and furious, came in like a whirlwind and stood on the corner of the carpet, with a broken basin in one hand and a threat in the other, which was clenched.

"Look 'ere!" she cried, "my only basin; and what the powers am I to make the beefsteak and kidney pudding in that your ma ordered for your dinners? You don't deserve no dinners, so yer don't."

"I'm awfully sorry, Cook," said Anthea gently. "It was my fault, and I forgot to tell you about it. It got broken when we were telling our fortunes with melted lead, you know, and I meant to tell you."

"Meant to tell me," replied the cook; she was red with anger, and really I don't wonder. "Meant to tell! Well, *I* mean to tell too. I've held my tongue this week through, because the missus she said to me quiet like, 'We mustn't expect old heads on young shoulders,' but now I shan't hold it no longer. There was the soap you put in our pudding, and me and Eliza never so much as breathed it to your ma— though well we might—and the saucepan, and the fish slice, and— My gracious cats alive! what 'ave you got that blessed child dressed up in his outdoors for?"

"We aren't going to take him out," said Anthea. "At least—" She stopped short, for though they weren't going to take him out in the Kentish Town Road, they certainly intended to take him elsewhere. But not all where Cook meant when she said "out." This confused the truthful Anthea.

"Out!" said the cook. "That I'll take care you don't." And she snatched the Lamb from the lap of Jane, while Anthea and Robert caught her by the skirts and apron.

"Look here," said Cyril in stern desperation, "will you go away and make your pudding in a pie dish, or a flowerpot, or a hot-water can, or something?"

"Not me," said the cook briefly. "And leave this precious poppet for you to give his deathercold to?"

"I warn you," said Cyril solemnly. "Beware, ere yet it be too late."

"Late yourself! The little popsey-wopsey," said the cook with angry tenderness. "They shan't take it out, no more they shan't. And— Where did you get that there yellow fowl?"

She pointed to the Phoenix.

Even Anthea saw that unless the cook lost her situation the loss would be theirs.

"I wish," she said suddenly, "we were on a sunny southern shore, where there can't be any whooping cough."

She said it through the frightened howls of the Lamb, and

the sturdy scoldings of the cook, and instantly the giddy-go-round-and-falling-lift feeling swept over the whole party, and the cook sat down flat on the carpet, holding the screaming Lamb tight to her stout print-covered self, and calling on St. Bridget to help her; she was an Irishwoman.

The moment the tipsy-topsy-turvey feeling stopped, the cook opened her eyes, gave one sounding screech and shut them again, and Anthea took the opportunity to get the desperately howling Lamb into her own arms.

"It's all right," she said, "own Panther's got you. Look at the trees, and the sand, and the shells, and the great big tortoises. Oh, *dear*, how hot it is!"

It certainly was; for the trusty carpet had laid itself out on a southern shore that was sunny and no mistake, as Robert remarked. The greenest of green slopes led up to glorious groves where palm trees and all the tropical flowers and fruits that you read of in *Westward Ho!* and *Foul Play* were growing in rich profusion. Between the green, green slope and the blue, blue sea, lay a stretch of sand that looked like a carpet of jeweled cloth of gold, for it was not grayish as our northern sand is, but yellow and changing—opal-colored like sunshine and rainbows. And at the very moment when the wild, whirling, blinding, deafening, tumbling upside-downness of the carpet-moving stopped, the children had the happiness of seeing three large live turtles waddle down to the edge of the sea and disappear in the water. And it was hotter than you can possibly imagine, unless you think of ovens on a baking day.

Everyone without an instant's hesitation tore off its London-in-November outdoor clothes, and Anthea took off the Lamb's highwayman blue coat and his three-cornered hat, and then his jersey, and then the Lamb himself suddenly slipped out of his little blue tight breeches and stood up happy and hot in his little white shirt.

"I'm sure it's much warmer than the seaside in the summer," said Anthea. "Mother always lets us go barefoot then."

So the Lamb's shoes and socks and gaiters came off, and he stood digging his happy naked pink toes into the golden smooth sand.

"I'm a little white duck-dickie," said he, "a little white duck-dickie what swims," and splashed quacking into the sandy pool.

"Let him," said Anthea. "It can't hurt him. Oh, how hot it is!"

The cook suddenly opened her eyes and screamed, shut them, screamed again, opened her eyes once more and said:

"Why, drat my cats alive, what's all this? It's a dream, I expect. Well, it's the best I ever dreamed. I'll look it up in the dreambook tomorrow. Seaside and trees and a carpet to sit on. I never did!"

"Look here," said Cyril, "it isn't a dream; it's real."

"Ho yes!" said the cook. "They always says that in dreams."

"It's REAL, I tell you," Robert said, stamping his foot. "I'm not going to tell you how it's done, because that's our secret." He winked heavily at each of the others in turn. "But you wouldn't go away and make that pudding, so we *had* to bring you, and I hope you like it."

"I do that, and no mistake," said the cook unexpectedly. "And it being a dream it don't matter what I say; and I *will* say, if it's my last word, that of all the aggravating little varmints—"

"Calm yourself, my good woman," said the Phoenix.

"Good woman, indeed," said the cook. "Good woman yourself!" Then she saw who it was that had spoken. "Well, if I ever," said she. "This is something like a dream! Yellow fowls a-talking and all! I've heard of such, but never did I think to see the day."

"Well, then," said Cyril impatiently, "sit here and see the day *now*. It's a jolly fine day. Here, you others—a council!"

They walked along the shore till they were out of earshot of the cook, who still sat gazing about her with a happy, dreamy, vacant smile.

"Look here," said Cyril, "we must roll the carpet up and hide it, so that we can get at it at any moment. The Lamb can be getting rid of his whooping cough all the morning, and we can look about; and if the savages on this island are cannibals we'll hook it and take her back. And if not, we'll *leave her here*."

"Is that being kind to servants and animals, like the clergyman said?" asked Jane.

"Nor she isn't kind," retorted Cyril.

"Well—anyway," said Anthea, "the safest thing is to leave the carpet there with her sitting on it. Perhaps it'll be a lesson to her, and anyway, if she thinks it's a dream it won't matter what she says when she gets home."

So the extra coats and hats and mufflers were piled on the carpet. Cyril shouldered the well and happy Lamb, the Phoenix perched on Robert's wrist, and the "party of explorers prepared to enter the interior."

The grassy slope was smooth, but under the trees there were tangled creepers with bright, strange-shaped flowers, and it was not easy to walk.

"We ought to have an explorer's axe," said Robert. "I shall ask Father to give me one for Christmas."

There were curtains of creepers with scented blossoms hanging from the trees, and brilliant birds darted about quite close to their faces.

"Now, tell me honestly," said the Phoenix, "are there any birds here handsomer than I am? Don't be afraid of hurting my feelings—I'm a modest bird, I hope."

"Not one of them," said Robert with conviction, "is a patch upon you!"

"I was never a vain bird," said the Phoenix, "but I own that you confirm my own impression. I will take a flight." It circled in the air for a moment, and returning to Robert's wrist, went on, "There is a path to the left."

And there was. So now the children went on through the wood more quickly and comfortably, the girls picking flowers and the Lamb inviting the "pretty dickies" to observe that he himself was a "little white real-water-wet duck!"

And all this time he hadn't whooping-coughed once.

The path turned and twisted, and, always threading their way amid a tangle of flowers, the children suddenly passed a corner and found themselves in a forest clearing, where there were a lot of pointed huts—the huts, as they knew at once, of *savages*.

The boldest heart beat more quickly. Suppose they *were* cannibals. It was a long way back to the carpet.

"Hadn't we better go back?" said Jane. "Go *now*," she said, and her voice trembled a little. "Suppose they eat us?"

"Nonsense, Pussy," said Cyril firmly. "Look, there's a goat tied up. That shows they don't eat *people*."

"Let's go on and say we're missionaries," Robert suggested.

"I shouldn't advise *that*," said the Phoenix very earnestly.

"Why not?"

"Well, for one thing, it isn't true," replied the golden bird.

It was while they stood hesitating on the edge of the clearing that a tall man suddenly came out of one of the huts. He had hardly any clothes, and his body all over was a dark and beautiful coppery color—just like the chrysanthemums Father had brought home on Saturday. In his hand he held a spear. The whites of his eyes and the white of his teeth were the only light things about him, except that where the sun shone on his shiny brown body it looked white too. If you will look carefully at the next shiny savage you meet with next to nothing on, you will see at once—if the sun happens to be shining at the time—that I am right about this.

The savage looked at the children. Concealment was impossible. He uttered a shout that was more like "Oo goggery bag-wag" than anything else the children had ever heard, and at once brown coppery people leapt out of every hut and swarmed like ants about the clearing. There was no time for discussion, and no one wanted to discuss anything, anyhow. Whether these coppery people were cannibals or not now seemed to matter very little.

Without an instant's hesitation the four children turned and ran back along the forest path; the only pause was Anthea's. She stood back to let Cyril pass, because he was carrying the Lamb, who screamed with delight. (He had not whooping-coughed a single once since the carpet landed him on the island.)

"Gee-up, Squirrel; gee-gee," he shouted, and Cyril did gee-up. The path was a shorter cut to the beach than the creeper-covered way by which they had come, and almost directly they saw through the trees the shining blue and gold and opal of sand and sea.

"Stick to it," cried Cyril breathlessly.

They did stick to it; they tore down the sands—they could hear behind them as they ran the patter of feet which they knew, too well, were copper-colored.

The sands were golden and opal-colored—*and bare*. There were wreaths of tropic seaweed, there were rich tropic shells of the kind you would not buy in the Kentish Town Road under at least fifteen pence a pair. There were turtles basking lumpily on the water's edge—but no cook, no clothes, and no carpet.

"On, on! Into the sea!" Cyril gasped. "They *must* hate water. I've—heard—savages always—dirty."

Their feet were splashing in the warm shallows before his breathless words were ended. The calm baby waves were easy to go through. It is warm work running for your life in the tropics, and the coolness of the water was delicious. They were up to their armpits now, and Jane was up to her chin.

"Look!" cried the Phoenix. "What are they pointing at?"

The children turned; and there, a little to the west, was a head—a head they knew, with a crooked cap upon it. It was the head of the cook.

For some reason or other the savages had stopped at the water's edge and were all talking at the top of their voices, and all were pointing copper-colored fingers, stiff with inter-est and excitement, at the head of the cook.

The children hurried toward her as quickly as the water would let them.

"What on earth did you come out here for?" Robert shouted. "And where on earth's the carpet?"

"It's not on earth, bless you," replied the cook happily. "It's *under me*—in the water. I got a bit warm setting there in the sun, and I just says, 'I wish I was in a cold bath' —just like that—and next minute here I was! It's all part of the dream."

Everyone at once saw how extremely fortunate it was that the carpet had had the sense to take the cook to the nearest and largest bath—the sea—and how terrible it would have been if the carpet had taken itself and her to the stuffy little bathroom of the house in Camden Town!

"Excuse me," said the Phoenix's soft voice, breaking in on the general sigh of relief, "but I think these brown people want your cook."

"To—to eat?" whispered Jane, as well as she could through the water which the plunging Lamb was dashing in her face with happy fat hands and feet.

"Hardly," rejoined the bird. "Who wants cooks to *eat*? Cooks are *engaged*, not eaten. They wish to engage her."

"How can you understand what they say?" asked Cyril doubtfully.

"It's as easy as kissing your claw," replied the bird. "I speak and understand *all* languages, even that of your cook, which is difficult and unpleasing. It's quite easy, when you know how it's done. It just comes to you. I should advise you to beach the carpet and land the cargo—the cook, I mean. You can take my word for it, the copper-colored ones will not harm you now."

It is impossible not to take the word of a Phoenix when it tells you to. So the children at once got hold of the corners of the carpet and, pulling it from under the cook, towed it slowly in through the shallowing water and at last spread it on the sand. The cook, who had followed, instantly sat down on it, and at once the copper-colored natives, now strangely humble, formed a ring round the carpet and fell on their faces on the rainbow-and-gold sand. The tallest savage spoke in this position, which must have been very awkward for him; and Jane noticed that it took him quite a long time to get the sand out of his mouth afterward.

"He says," the Phoenix remarked after some time, "that they wish to engage your cook permanently."

"Without a character*?" asked Anthea, who had heard her mother speak of such things.

"They do not wish to engage her as cook, but as *queen*; and queens need not have characters."

There was a breathless pause.

"*Well,*" said Cyril, "of all the choices! But there's no accounting for tastes."

Everyone laughed at the idea of the cook's being engaged as queen; they could not help it.

"I do not advise laughter," warned the Phoenix, ruffling out his golden feathers, which were extremely wet. "And it's not their own choice. It seems that there is an ancient prophecy of this copper-colored tribe that a great queen should someday arise out of the sea with a white crown on her head, and—and—well, you see! There's the crown!"

It pointed its claw at cook's cap; and a very dirty cap it was, because it was the end of the week.

---

*Character reference

"That's the white crown," it said. "At least, it's nearly white—very white indeed compared to the color *they* are—and anyway, it's quite white enough."

Cyril addressed the cook. "Look here!" said he. "These brown people want you to be their queen. They're only savages, and they don't know any better. Now would you really like to stay? Or, if you'll promise not to be so jolly aggravating at home, and not to tell anyone a word about today, we'll take you back to Camden Town."

"No, you don't," said the cook in firm, undoubting tones. "I've always wanted to be the Queen, God bless her! and I always thought what a good one I should make; and now I'm going to. *If* it's only in a dream, it's well worth while. And I don't go back to that nasty underground kitchen, and me blamed for everything; that I don't, not till the dream's finished and I wake up with that nasty bell a rang-tanging in my ears—so I tell you."

"Are you *sure*," Anthea anxiously asked the Phoenix, "that she will be quite safe here?"

"She will find the nest of a queen a very precious and soft thing," said the bird solemnly.

"There—you hear," said Cyril. "You're in for a precious soft thing, so mind you're a good queen, Cook. It's more than you'd any right to expect, but long may you reign."

Some of the cook's copper-colored subjects now advanced from the forest with long garlands of beautiful flowers, white and sweet-scented, and hung them respectfully round the neck of their new sovereign.

"What! All them lovely bokays for me!" exclaimed the enraptured cook. "Well! This here is something *like* a dream, I must say."

She sat up very straight on the carpet, and the copper-colored ones, themselves wreathed in garlands of the gayest flowers, madly stuck parrot feathers in their hair and began to dance. It was a dance such as you have never seen; it made the children feel almost sure that the cook was right, and that they were all in a dream. Small, strange-shaped drums were beaten, odd-sounding songs were sung, and the dance got faster and faster and odder and odder, till at last all the dancers fell on the sand tired out.

The new queen, with her white crown-cap all on one side, clapped wildly.

"Brayvo!" she cried. "Brayvo! It's better than the Albert Edward Music-hall in the Kentish Town Road. Go it again!"

But the Phoenix would not translate this request into the copper-colored language; and when the savages had recovered their breath, they implored their queen to leave her white escort and come with them to their huts.

"The finest shall be yours, O Queen," said they.

"Well—so long!" said the cook, getting heavily onto her feet, when the Phoenix had translated this request. "No more kitchens and attics for me, thank you. I'm off to my royal palace. I am; and I only wish this here dream would keep on forever and ever."

She picked up the ends of the garlands that trailed round her feet and the children had one last glimpse of her striped stockings and worn elastic-side boots before she disappeared into the shadow of the forest, surrounded by her dusky retainers, singing songs of rejoicing as they went.

"Well!" said Cyril. "I suppose she's all right, but they don't seem to count us for much, one way or the other."

"Oh," said the Phoenix, "they think you're merely dreams.

The prophecy said that the queen would arise from the waves with a white crown and surrounded by white dream-children. That's about what they think *you* are!"

"And what about dinner?" said Robert abruptly.

"There won't be any dinner, with no cook and no pudding basin," Anthea reminded him. "But there's always bread and butter."

"Let's get home," said Cyril.

The Lamb was furiously unwishful to be dressed in his warm clothes again, but Anthea and Jane managed it, by force disguised as coaxing, and he never once whooping-coughed.

Then everyone put on its own warm things and took its place on the carpet.

A sound of uncouth singing still came from beyond the trees, where the copper-colored natives were crooning songs of admiration and respect to their white-crowned queen. Then Anthea said, "Home," just as duchesses and other people do to their coachmen, and the intelligent carpet in one whirling moment laid itself down in its proper place on the nursery floor. And at that very moment Eliza opened the door and said:

"Cook's gone! I can't find her anywhere, and there's no dinner ready. She hasn't taken her box nor yet her outdoor things. She just ran out to see the time, I shouldn't wonder—the kitchen clock never did give her any satisfaction—and she's got run over or fell down in a fit as likely as not. You'll have to put up with the cold bacon for your dinners; and what on earth you've got your outdoor things on for I don't know. And then I'll slip out and see if they know anything about her at the police station."

But nobody ever knew anything about the cook any more, except the children and, later, one other person.

Mother was so upset at losing the cook, and so anxious about her, that Anthea felt most miserable, as though she had done something very wrong indeed. She woke several times in the night, and at last decided that she would ask the Phoenix to let her tell her mother all about it. But there was no opportunity to do this next day, because the Phoenix, as usual, had gone to sleep in some out-of-the-way spot, after asking, as a special favor, not to be disturbed for twenty-four hours.

The Lamb never whooping-coughed once all that Sunday, and Mother and Father said what good medicine it was that the doctor had given him. But the children knew that it was the southern shore where you can't have whooping-cough that had cured him. The Lamb babbled of colored sand and water, but no one took any notice of that. He often talked of things that hadn't happened.

It was on Monday morning, very early indeed, that Anthea woke and suddenly made up her mind. She crept downstairs in her nightgown (it was very chilly), sat down on the carpet, and with a beating heart wished herself on the sunny shore where you can't have whooping-cough, and next moment there she was.

The sand was splendidly warm. She could feel it at once, even through the carpet. She folded the carpet and put it over her shoulders like a shawl, for she was determined not to be parted from it for a single instant, no matter how hot it might be to wear.

Then trembling a little, and trying to keep up her courage

by saying over and over, "It is my *duty*, it *is* my duty," she
went up the forest path.

"Well, here you are again," said the cook, directly she saw
Anthea. "This dream does keep on!"

The cook was dressed in a white robe; she had no shoes
and stockings and no cap, and she was sitting under a screen
of palm leaves, for it was afternoon in the island, and blazing
hot. She wore a flower wreath on her hair, and copper-
colored boys were fanning her with peacocks' feathers.

"They've got the cap put away," she said. "They seem to
think a lot of it. Never saw one before, I expect."

"Are you happy?" asked Anthea, panting; the sight of the
cook as queen took her breath away.

"I believe you, my dear," said the cook heartily. "Nothing
to do unless you want to. But I'm getting rested now. Tomorrow I'm going to start cleaning out my hut, if the dream
keeps on, and I shall teach them cooking; they burns everything to a cinder now unless they eats it raw."

"But can you talk to them?"

"Lor' love a duck, yes!" the happy cook-queen replied.
"It's quite easy to pick up. I always thought I should be quick
at foreign languages. I've taught them to understand 'dinner,'
and 'I want a drink,' and 'You leave me be,' already."

"Then you don't want anything," Anthea asked earnestly
and anxiously.

"Not me, miss; except if you'd only go away. I'm afraid of
me waking up with that bell a-going if you keep on stopping
there a-talking to me. Long as this here dream keeps up I'm as
happy as a queen."

"Good-bye, then," said Anthea gaily, for her conscience
was clear now.

She hurried into the wood, threw herself on the ground, and said "Home"—and there she was, rolled in the carpet on the nursery floor.

"*She's* all right, anyhow," said Anthea, and went back to bed. "I'm glad somebody's pleased. But Mother will never believe me when I tell her."

The story is indeed a little difficult to believe. Still, you might try.

# Chapter 4

# Two Bazaars

*M*other was really a great dear. She was pretty and she was loving, and most frightfully good when you were ill, and always kind, and almost always just. That is, she was just when she understood things. But of course she did not always understand things. No one understands everything, and mothers are not angels, though a good many of them come pretty near it. The children knew that Mother always *wanted* to do what was best for them, even if she was not clever enough to know exactly what was the best. That was why all of them, but much more particularly Anthea, felt rather uncomfortable at keeping the great secret from her of the wishing carpet and the Phoenix. And Anthea, whose inside mind was made so that she was able to be much more uncomfortable than the others, had decided that she *must* tell her mother the truth, however little likely it was that her mother would believe it.

"Then I shall have done what's right," said she to the Phoenix. "And if she doesn't believe me it won't be my fault—will it?"

"Not in the least," said the golden bird. "And she won't, so you're quite safe."

Anthea chose a time when she was doing her home lessons—they were Algebra and Latin, German, English, and Euclid—and she asked her mother whether she might come and do them in the drawing room—"so as to be quiet," she said to her mother; and to herself she said, "And that's not the real reason. I hope I shan't grow up a *liar*."

Mother said, "Of course, dearie," and Anthea started swimming through a sea of $x$'s and $y$'s and $z$'s. Mother was sitting at the mahogany bureau writing letters.

"Mother dear," said Anthea.

"Yes, love-a-duck," said Mother.

"About Cook," said Anthea. "*I* know where she is."

"Do you, dear?" said Mother. "Well, I wouldn't take her back after the way she has behaved."

"It's not her fault," said Anthea. "May I tell you about it from the beginning?"

Mother laid down her pen, and her nice face had a resigned expression. As you know, a resigned expression always makes you want not to tell anybody anything.

"It's like this," said Anthea, in a hurry. "That egg, you know, that came in the carpet; we put it in the fire and it hatched into the Phoenix, and the carpet was a wishing carpet—and—"

"A very nice game, darling," said Mother, taking up her pen. "Now do be quiet. I've got a lot of letters to write. I'm going to Bournemouth tomorrow with the Lamb—and there's that bazaar."

Anthea went back to $x,y,z$, and Mother's pen scratched busily.

"But, Mother," said Anthea, when Mother put down the pen to lick an envelope, "the carpet takes us wherever we like—and—"

"I wish it would take you where you could get a few nice Eastern things for my bazaar," said Mother. "I promised them, and I've no time to go to Liberty's now."

"It shall," said Anthea, "but Mother . . ."

"Well, dear," said Mother a little impatiently, for she had taken up her pen again.

"The carpet took us to a place where you couldn't have whooping-cough, and the Lamb hasn't whooped since, and we took Cook because she was so tiresome, and then she would stay and be queen of the savages. They thought her cap was a crown, and—"

"Darling one," said Mother, "you know I love to hear the things you make up—but I am most awfully busy."

"But it's true," said Anthea desperately.

"You shouldn't say that, my sweet," said Mother gently. And then Anthea knew it was hopeless.

"Are you going away for long?" asked Anthea.

"I've got a cold," said Mother, "and Daddy's anxious about it, and the Lamb's cough."

"He hasn't coughed since Saturday," the Lamb's eldest sister interrupted.

"I wish I could think so," Mother replied. "And Daddy's got to go to Scotland. I do hope you'll be good children."

"We will, we will," said Anthea fervently. "When's the bazaar?"

"On Saturday," said Mother, "at the schools. Oh, don't talk any more, there's a treasure! My head's going round, and I've forgotten how to spell whooping-cough."

*    *    *

Mother and the Lamb went away, and Father went away, and there was a new cook who looked so like a frightened rabbit that no one had the heart to do anything to frighten her any more than seemed natural to her.

The Phoenix begged to be excused. It said it wanted a week's rest, and asked that it might not be disturbed. And it hid its golden gleaming self, and nobody could find it.

So that when Wednesday afternoon brought an unexpected holiday and everyone decided to go somewhere on the carpet, the journey had to be undertaken without the Phoenix. They were debarred from any carpet excursions in the evening by a sudden promise to Mother, exacted in the agitation of parting, that they would not be out after six at night, except on Saturday, when they were to go to the bazaar, and were pledged to put on their best clothes, to wash themselves to the uttermost, and to clean their nails—not with scissors, which are scratchy and bad, but with flat-sharpened ends of wooden matches, which do no harm to anyone's nails.

"Let's go and see the Lamb," said Jane.

But everyone was agreed that if they appeared suddenly in Bournemouth it would frighten Mother out of her wits, if not into a fit. So they sat on the carpet, and thought and thought and thought till they almost began to squint.

"Look here," said Cyril, "I know. Please, carpet, take us somewhere where we can see the Lamb and Mother and no one can see us."

"Except the Lamb," said Jane quickly.

And the next moment they found themselves recovering from the upside-down movement—and there they were sitting on the carpet, and the carpet was laid out over another thick soft carpet of brown pine needles. There were green pine trees overhead, and a swift clear little stream was running as fast as ever it could between steep banks—and there, sitting on the pine-needle carpet, was Mother, without her hat; and the sun was shining brightly, although it was November—and there was the Lamb, as jolly as jolly and not whooping at all.

"The carpet's deceived us," said Robert gloomily. "Mother will see us directly she turns her head."

But the faithful carpet had not deceived them.

Mother turned her dear head and looked straight at them, and *did not see them!*

"We're invisible," Cyril whispered. "What awful larks!"

But to the girls it was not larks at all. It was horrible to have Mother looking straight at them, and her face keeping the same, just as though they weren't there.

"I don't like it," said Jane. "Mother never looked at us like that before. Just as if she didn't love us—as if we were somebody else's children, and not very nice ones either—as if she didn't care whether she saw us or not."

"It *is* horrid," said Anthea, almost in tears.

But at this moment the Lamb saw them, and plunged toward the carpet, shrieking "Panty, own Panty—an' Pussy an' Squiggle—an' Bobs, oh, oh!"

Anthea caught him and kissed him, so did Jane; they could not help it—he looked such a darling, with his blue three-cornered hat all on one side, and his precious face all dirty—quite in the old familiar way.

"I love you, Panty; I love you—and you, and you, and you," cried the Lamb.

It was a delicious moment. Even the boys thumped their baby brother joyously on the back.

Then Anthea glanced at Mother—and mother's face was a pale sea-green color, and she was staring at the Lamb as if she thought he had gone mad. And, indeed, that was exactly what she did think.

"My Lamb, my precious! Come to Mother," she cried, and jumped up and ran to the baby.

She was so quick that the invisible children had to leap back, or she would have felt them; and to feel what you can't see is the worst sort of ghost-feeling. Mother picked up the Lamb and hurried away from the pine wood.

"Let's go home," said Jane, after a miserable silence. "It feels just exactly as if Mother didn't love us."

But they couldn't bear to go home till they had seen Mother meet another lady, and knew that she was safe. You cannot leave your mother to go green in the face in a distant pine wood, far from all human aid, and then go home on your wishing carpet as though nothing had happened.

When Mother seemed safe the children returned to the carpet and said "Home"—and home they went.

"I don't care about being invisible, myself," said Cyril, "at least, not with my own family. It would be different if you were a prince, or a bandit, or a burglar."

And now the thoughts of all four dwelt fondly on the dear greenish face of mother.

"I wish she hadn't gone away," said Jane. "The house is simply beastly without her."

"I think we ought to do what she said," Anthea put in. "I saw something in a book the other day about the wishes of the departed being sacred."

"That means when they've departed farther off," said Cyril. "Indian's coral or Greenland's icy, don't you know; not Bournemouth. Besides, we don't know what her wishes are."

"She *said*"—Anthea was very much inclined to cry—"she said, 'Get Indian things for my bazaar,' but I know she thought we couldn't and it was only play."

"Let's get them all the same," said Robert. "We'll go the first thing on Saturday morning."

And on Saturday morning, the first thing, they went.

There was no finding the Phoenix, so they sat on the beautiful wishing carpet, and said:

"We want Indian things for Mother's bazaar. Will you please take us where people will give us heaps of Indian things?"

The docile carpet swirled their senses away and restored them on the outskirts of a gleaming white Indian town. They knew it was Indian at once, by the shape of the domes and roofs; and besides, a man went by on an elephant, and two English soldiers went along the road, talking like in Mr. Kipling's books—so after that no one could have any doubt as to where they were. They rolled up the carpet and Robert carried it, and they walked boldly into town. It was very warm, and once more they had to take off their London-in-November coats and carry them on their arms.

The streets were narrow and strange, and the clothes of the people in the streets were strange, and the talk of the people was strangest of all.

"I can't understand a word," said Cyril. "How on earth are we to ask for things for our bazaar?"

"And they're poor people, too," said Jane. "I'm sure they are. What we want is a rajah or something."

Robert was beginning to unroll the carpet, but the others stopped him, imploring him not to waste a wish.

"We asked the carpet to take us where we could get Indian things for bazaars," said Anthea, "and it will."

Her faith was justified.

Just as she finished speaking a very brown gentleman in a turban came up to them and bowed deeply. He spoke, and they thrilled to the sound of English words.

"My ranee, she think you very nice childs. She asks do you lose yourselves, and do you desire to sell carpet? She see you from her palkee. You come see her—yes?"

They followed the stranger, who seemed to have a great many more teeth in his smile than are usual, and led them through crooked streets to the ranee's palace. I am not going to describe the ranee's palace, because I really have never seen the palace of a ranee, and Mr. Kipling has. So you can read about it in his books. But I know exactly what happened there.

The old ranee sat on a low-cushioned seat, and there were a lot of other ladies with her—all in trousers and veils, and sparkling with tinsel and gold and jewels. And the brown, turbaned gentleman stood behind a sort of carved screen, and interpreted what the children said and what the queen said. And when the queen asked to buy the carpet, the children said "No."

"Why?" asked the ranee.

And Jane briefly said why, and the interpreter interpreted. The queen spoke, and then the interpreter said:

"My mistress says it is a good story, and you tell it all through without thought of time."

And they had to. It made a long story, especially as it had

all to be told twice—once by Cyril and once by the interpreter. Cyril rather enjoyed himself. He warmed to his work, and told the tale of the Phoenix and the Carpet, and the Lone Tower, and the Queen-Cook, in language that grew insensibly more and more Arabian Nightsy, and the ranee and her ladies listened to the interpreter, and rolled about on their fat cushions with laughter.

When the story was ended she spoke, and the interpreter explained that she had said, "Little one, thou art a heaven-born teller of tales"; and she threw him a string of turquoises from round her neck.

"Oh, how lovely!" cried Jane and Anthea.

Cyril bowed several times, and then cleared his throat and said:

"Thank her very, very much; but I would much rather she gave me some of the cheap things in the bazaar. Tell her I want them to sell again, and give the money to buy clothes for poor people who haven't any."

"Tell him he has my leave to sell my gift and clothe the naked with its price," said the queen, when this was translated.

But Cyril said very firmly, "No thank you. The things have got to be sold today at our bazaar, and no one would buy a turquoise necklace at an English bazaar. They'd think it was sham, or else they'd want to know where we got it."

So then the queen sent out for little pretty things, and her servants piled the carpet with them.

"I must needs lend you an elephant to carry them away," she said, laughing.

But Anthea said, "If the queen will lend us a comb and let us wash our hands and faces, she shall see a magic thing. We and the carpet and all these brass trays and pots and carved

things and stuffs and things will just vanish away like
smoke."

The queen clapped her hands at this idea, and lent the
children a sandalwood comb inlaid with ivory lotus flowers.
And they washed their faces and hands in silver basins.

Then Cyril made a very polite farewell speech, and quite
suddenly he ended with the words:

"And I wish we were at the bazaar at our schools."

And of course they were. And the queen and her ladies
were left with their mouths open, gazing at the bare space on
the inlaid marble floor where the carpet and the children
had been.

"That is magic, if ever magic was," said the queen, delighted
with the incident; which, indeed, has given the ladies of
that court something to talk about on wet days ever since.

Cyril's stories had taken some time, so had the meal of
strange sweet foods that they had had while the little pretty
things were being bought, and the gas in the schoolroom was
already lighted. Outside, the winter dusk was stealing down
among the Camden Town houses.

"I'm glad we got washed in India," said Cyril. "We should
have been awfully late if we'd had to go home and scrub."

"Besides," Robert said, "it's much warmer washing in
India. I shouldn't mind it so much if we lived there."

The thoughtful carpet had dumped the children down in a
dusky space behind the point where the corners of two stalls
met. The floor was littered with string and brown paper, and
baskets and boxes were heaped along the wall.

The children crept out under a stall covered with all sorts
of table covers and mats and things, embroidered beautifully
by idle ladies with no real work to do. They got out at the

end, displacing a sideboard cloth adorned with a tasteful pattern of blue geraniums. The girls got out unobserved, so did Cyril, but Robert, as he cautiously emerged, was actually walked on by Mrs. Biddle, who kept the stall. Her large, solid foot stood firmly on the small, solid hand of Robert— and who can blame Robert, if he *did* yell a little?

A crowd instantly collected. Yells are very unusual at bazaars, and everyone was intensely interested. It was several seconds before the three free children could make Mrs. Biddle understand that what she was walking on was not a schoolroom floor, or even, as she presently supposed, a dropped pin cushion, but the living hand of a suffering child. When she became aware that she really had hurt him, she grew very angry indeed. When people have hurt other people by accident, the one who does the hurting is always much the angriest. I wonder why.

"I'm very sorry, I'm sure," said Mrs. Biddle; but she spoke more in anger than in sorrow. "Come out! Whatever do you mean by creeping about under the stalls, like earwigs?"

"We were looking at the things in the corner."

"Such nasty, prying ways," said Mrs. Biddle, "will never make you successful in life. There's nothing there but packing and dust."

"Oh, isn't there!" said Jane. "That's all you know."

"Little girl, don't be rude," said Mrs. Biddle, flushing violet.

"She doesn't mean to be; but there *are* some nice things there, all the same," said Cyril; who suddenly felt how impossible it was to inform the listening crowd that all the treasures piled on the carpet were Mother's contributions to the bazaar. No one would believe it; and if they did, and wrote to thank Mother, she would think—well, goodness only knew what she would think. The other three children felt the same.

"I should like to see them," said a very nice lady, whose friends had disappointed her and who hoped that these might be belated contributions to her poorly furnished stall.

She looked inquiringly at Robert, who said, "With pleasure, don't mention it," and dived back under Mrs. Biddle's stall.

"I wonder you encourage such behavior," said Mrs. Biddle. "I always speak my mind, as you know, Miss Peasmarsh; and, I must say, I am surprised." She turned to the crowd. "There is no entertainment here," she said sternly. "A very naughty little boy has accidentally hurt himself, but only slightly. Will you please disperse? It will only encourage him in naughtiness if he finds himself the center of attraction."

The crowd slowly dispersed. Anthea, speechless with fury, heard a nice curate say "Poor little beggar!" and loved the curate at once and forever.

Then Robert wriggled out from under the stall with some Benares brass and some inlaid sandalwood boxes.

"Liberty!" cried Miss Peasmarsh. "Then Charles has not forgotten, after all."

"Excuse me," said Mrs. Biddle with fierce politeness, "these objects are deposited behind *my* stall. Some unknown donor who does good by stealth and would blush if he could hear you claim the things. Of course they are for me."

"My stall touches yours at the corner," said poor Miss Peasmarsh, timidly, "and my cousin did promise—"

The children sidled away from the unequal contest and

mingled with the crowd. Their feelings were too deep for words—till at last Robert said:

"That stiff-starched *pig!*"

"And after all our trouble! I'm hoarse with gassing to that trousered lady in India."

"The pig-lady's very, very nasty," said Jane.

It was Anthea who said, in a hurried undertone, "She isn't very nice, and Miss Peasmarsh is pretty and nice too. Who's got a pencil?"

It was a long crawl, under three stalls, but Anthea did it. A large piece of pale blue paper lay among the rubbish in the corner. She folded it to a square and wrote upon it, licking the pencil at every word to make it mark quite blackly: "All these Indian things are for pretty, nice Miss Peasmarsh's stall." She thought of adding, "There is nothing for Mrs. Biddle," but she saw that this might lead to suspicion, so she wrote hastily: "From an unknown donna," and crept back among the boards and trestles to join the others.

So that when Mrs. Biddle appealed to the bazaar committee, and the corner of the stall was lifted and shifted, so that stout clergymen and heavy ladies could get to the corner without creeping under stalls, the blue paper was discovered, and all the splendid, shining Indian things were given over to Miss Peasmarsh, and she sold them all, and got thirty-five pounds for them.

"I don't understand about the blue paper," said Mrs. Biddle. "It looks to me like the work of a lunatic. And saying you were nice and pretty! It's not the work of a sane person."

Anthea and Jane begged Miss Peasmarsh to let them help her to sell the things, because it was their brother who had announced the good news that the things had come. Miss

Peasmarsh was very willing, for now her stall, which had been so neglected, was surrounded by people who wanted to buy, and she was glad to be helped. The children noted that Mrs. Biddle had not more to do in the way of selling than she could manage quite well. I hope they were not glad—for you should forgive your enemies, even if they walk on your hands and then say it is all your naughty fault. But I am afraid they were not so sorry as they ought to have been.

It took some time to arrange the things on the stall. The carpet was spread over it, and the dark colors showed up the brass and silver and ivory things. It was a happy and busy afternoon, and when Miss Peasmarsh and the girls had sold every single one of the little pretty things from the Indian bazaar, far, far away, Anthea and Jane went off with the boys to fish in the fishpond, and dive into the bran pie, and hear the cardboard band, and the phonograph, and the chorus of singing birds that was done behind a screen with glass tubes and glasses of water.

They had a beautiful tea, suddenly presented to them by the nice curate, and Miss Peasmarsh joined them before they had had more than three cakes each. It was a merry party, and the curate was extremely pleasant to everyone, "even to Miss Peasmarsh," as Jane said afterward.

"We ought to get back to the stall," said Anthea, when no one could possibly eat any more and the curate was talking in a low voice to Miss Peasmarsh about "after Easter."

"There's nothing to go back for," said Miss Peasmarsh gaily. "Thanks to you dear children we've sold everything."

"There's—there's the carpet," said Cyril.

"Oh," said Miss Peasmarsh radiantly, "don't bother about the carpet. I've sold even that. Mrs. Biddle gave me ten shillings for it. She said it would do for her servants' bedroom."

"Why," said Jane, "her servants don't *have* carpets. We had Cook from her, and she told us so."

"No scandal about Queen Elizabeth, if *you* please," said the curate cheerfully; and Miss Peasmarsh laughed, and looked at him as though she had never dreamed that any one *could* be so amusing. But the others were struck dumb. How could they say "The carpet is ours!" For who brings carpets to bazaars?

The children were now thoroughly wretched. But I am glad to say that their wretchedness did not make them forget their manners, as it does sometimes, even with grown-up people, who ought to know ever so much better.

They said, "Thank you very much for the jolly tea," and "Thanks for being so jolly," and "Thanks awfully for giving us such a jolly time"; for the curate had stood fishponds, and bran pies, and phonographs, and the chorus of singing birds, and had stood them like a man. The girls hugged Miss Peasmarsh, and as they went away they heard the curate say:

"Jolly little kids, yes, but what about—you will let it be directly after Easter? Ah, do say you will—"

And Jane ran back and said, before Anthea could drag her away, "What are you going to do after Easter?"

Miss Peasmarsh smiled and looked very pretty indeed. And the curate said:

"I hope I am going to take a trip to the Fortunate Islands."

"I wish we could take you on the wishing carpet," said Jane.

"Thank you," said the curate, "but I'm afraid I can't wait

for that. I must go to the Fortunate Islands before they make me a bishop. I should have no time afterward."

"I've always thought I should marry a bishop," said Jane. "His aprons would come in so useful. Wouldn't *you* like to marry a bishop, Miss Peasmarsh?"

It was then that they dragged her away.

As it was Robert's hand that Mrs. Biddle had walked on, it was decided that he had better not recall the incident to her mind, and so make her angry again. Anthea and Jane had helped to sell things at the rival stall, so they were not likely to be popular.

A hasty council of four decided that Mrs. Biddle would hate Cyril less than she would hate the others, so the others mingled with the crowd, and it was he who said to her:

"Mrs. Biddle, *we* meant to have that carpet. Would you sell it to us? We would give you—"

"Certainly not," said Mrs. Biddle. "Go away, little boy."

There was that in her tone which showed Cyril, all too plainly, the hopelessness of persuasion. He found the others and said:

"It's no use; she's like a lioness robbed of its puppies. We must watch where it goes—and—Anthea, I don't care what you say. It's our own carpet. It wouldn't be burglary. It would be a sort of forlorn hope rescue party—heroic and daring and dashing, and not wrong at all."

The children still wandered among the gay crowd—but there was no pleasure there for them anymore. The chorus of singing birds sounded just like glass tubes being blown through water, and the phonograph simply made a horrid noise, so that you could hardly hear yourself speak. And the people were buying things they couldn't possibly want, and it all seemed very stupid. And Mrs. Biddle had bought the wishing carpet for ten shillings. And the whole of life was sad and gray and dusty, and smelled of slight gas escapes, and hot people, and cake and crumbs, and all the children were very tired indeed.

They found a corner within sight of the carpet, and there they waited miserably, till it was far beyond their proper bedtime. And when it was ten the people who had bought things went away, but the people who had been selling stayed to count up their money.

"And to jaw about it," said Robert. "I'll never go to another bazaar as long as I ever live. My hand is swollen as big as a pudding. I expect the nails in her horrible boots were poisoned."

Just then someone who seemed to have a right to interfere said: "Everything is over now; you had better go home."

So they went. And then they waited on the pavement under the gas lamp, where ragged children had been standing all the evening to listen to the band, and their feet slipped about in the greasy mud till Mrs. Biddle came out, and was driven away in a cab with the many things she hadn't sold and the few things she had bought—among others the carpet. The other stall-holders left their things at the school till Monday morning, but Mrs. Biddle was afraid someone would steal some of them, so she took them in a cab.

The children, now too desperate to care for mud or appearances, hung on behind the cab till it reached Mrs. Biddle's house. When she and the carpet had gone in and the door was shut, Anthea said:

"Don't let's burgle—I mean do daring and dashing rescue

acts, till we've given her a chance. Let's ring and ask to see her."

The others hated to do this, but at last they agreed, on condition that Anthea would not make any silly fuss about the burglary afterward, if it really had to come to that.

So they knocked and rang, and a scared-looking parlor-maid opened the front door. While they were asking for Mrs. Biddle they saw her. She was in the dining room, and she had already pushed back the table and spread out the carpet to see how it looked on the floor.

"I knew she didn't want it for her servants' bedroom," Jane muttered.

Anthea walked straight past the uncomfortable parlor-maid, and the others followed her. Mrs. Biddle had her back to them and was smoothing down the carpet with the same boot that had trampled on the hand of Robert. So that they were all in the room, and Cyril, with great presence of mind, had shut the room door, before she saw them.

"Who is it, Jane?" she asked in a sour voice; and then, turning suddenly, she saw who it was. Once more her face grew violet—a deep, dark violet. "You wicked daring little things!" she cried. "How dare you come here? At this time of night too. Be off, or I'll send for the police."

"Don't be angry," Anthea said soothingly, "we only wanted to ask you to let us have the carpet. We have quite twelve shillings between us, and—"

"How *dare* you?" cried Mrs. Biddle, and her voice shook with angriness.

"You do look horrid," said Jane suddenly.

Mrs. Biddle actually stamped that booted foot of hers.

"You rude, barefaced child," she said.

Anthea almost shook Jane; but Jane pushed forward in spite of her.

"It really *is* our nursery carpet," she said. "You ask *anyone* if it isn't."

"Let's wish ourselves home," said Cyril in a whisper.

"No go," Robert whispered back, "she'd be there too, and raving mad as likely as not. Horrid thing. I hate her."

"I wish Mrs. Biddle was in an angelic good temper," cried Anthea suddenly. "It's worth trying," she said to herself.

Mrs. Biddle's face grew from purple to violet, and from violet to mauve, and from mauve to pink. Then she smiled quite a jolly smile.

"Why, so I am!" she said. "What a funny idea! Why shouldn't I be in a good temper, my dears?"

Once more the carpet had done its work, and not on Mrs. Biddle alone. The children felt suddenly good and happy.

"You're a jolly good sort," said Cyril. "I see that now. I'm sorry we vexed you at the bazaar today."

"Not another word," said the changed Mrs. Biddle. "Of course you shall have the carpet, my dears, if you've taken such a fancy to it. No. no; I won't have more than the ten shillings I paid."

"It does seem hard to ask you for it after you bought it at the bazaar," said Anthea, "but it really *is* our nursery carpet. It got to the bazaar by mistake, with some other things."

"Did it really, now? How vexing," said Mrs. Biddle kindly. "Well, my dears, I can very well give the extra ten shillings; so you take your carpet and we'll say no more about it. Have a piece of cake before you go! I'm so sorry I stepped on your hand, my boy. Is it all right now?"

"Yes, thank you," said Robert. "I say, you *are* good."

"Not at all," said Mrs. Biddle heartily. "I'm delighted to be able to give any little pleasure to you dear children."

And she helped them to roll up the carpet, and the boys carried it away between them.

"You *are* a dear," said Anthea, and she and Mrs. Biddle kissed each other heartily.

"*Well!*" said Cyril as they went along the street.

"Yes," said Robert, "and the odd part is that you feel just as if it was *real*—her being so jolly, I mean—and not only the carpet making her nice."

"Perhaps it *is* real," said Anthea, "only it was covered up with crossness and tiredness and things, and the carpet took them away."

"I hope it'll keep them away," said Jane, "she isn't ugly at all when she laughs."

The carpet has done many wonders in its day; but the case of Mrs. Biddle is, I think, the most wonderful. For from that day she was never anything like so disagreeable as she was before, and she sent a lovely silver teapot and a kind letter to Miss Peasmarsh when the pretty lady married the nice curate; just after Easter it was, and they went to Italy for their honeymoon.

# Chapter 5

# The Temple

**"I** wish we could find the Phoenix," said Jane. "It's much better company than the carpet."

"Beastly ungrateful, little kids are," said Cyril.

"No, I'm not; only the carpet never says anything, and it's so helpless. It doesn't seem able to take care of itself. It gets sold, and taken into the sea, and things like that. You wouldn't catch the Phoenix getting sold."

It was two days after the bazaar. Everyone was a little cross—some days are like that, usually Mondays by the way. And this was a Monday.

"I shouldn't wonder if your precious Phoenix had gone off for good," said Cyril. "And I don't know that I blame it. Look at the weather!"

"It's not worth looking at," said Robert. And indeed it wasn't.

"The Phoenix hasn't gone—I'm sure it hasn't," said Anthea. "I'll have another look for it."

Anthea looked under tables and chairs, and in boxes and baskets, in mother's workbag and father's portmanteau, but still the Phoenix showed not so much as the tip of one shining feather.

Then suddenly Robert remembered how the whole of the Greek invocation song of seven thousand lines had been condensed by him into one English hexameter, so he stood on the carpet and chanted:

"Oh, come along, you good old beautiful Phoenix"

and almost at once there was a rustle of wings down the kitchen stairs, and the Phoenix sailed in on wide gold wings.

"Where on earth *have* you been?" asked Anthea. "I've looked everywhere for you."

"Not *everywhere*," replied the bird, "because you did not look in the place where I was. Confess that that hallowed spot was overlooked by you."

"*What* hallowed spot?" asked Cyril, a little impatiently, for time was hastening on and the wishing carpet still idle.

"The spot," said the Phoenix, "which I hallowed by my golden presence was the Lutron."

"The *what?*"

"The bath—the place of washing."

"I'm sure you weren't," said Jane. "I looked there three times and moved all the towels."

"I was concealed," said the Phoenix, "on the summit of a metal column—enchanted, I should judge, for it felt warm to my golden toes, as though the glorious sun of the desert shone ever upon it."

"Oh, you mean the cylinder," said Cyril. "It *has* rather a comforting feel, this weather. And now where shall we go?"

And then, of course, the usual discussion broke out as to

where they should go and what they should do. And naturally, everyone wanted to do something that the others did
not care about.

"I am the eldest," Cyril remarked. "Let's go to the North
Pole."

"This weather! Likely!" Robert rejoined. "Let's go to the
equator."

"I think the diamond mines of Golconda would be nice,"
said Anthea. "Don't you agree, Jane?"

"No, I don't," retorted Jane. "I don't agree with you. I
don't agree with anybody."

The Phoenix raised a warning claw.

"If you cannot agree among yourselves, I fear I shall have
to leave you," it said.

"Well, where shall we go? You decide!" said all.

"If I were you," said the bird thoughtfully, "I should give
the carpet a rest. Besides, you'll lose the use of your legs if
you go everywhere by carpet. Can't you take me out and
explain your ugly city to me?"

"We will if it clears up," said Robert without enthusiasm.
"Just look at the rain. And why should we give the carpet a
rest?"

"Are you greedy and grasping, and heartless and selfish?"
asked the bird sharply.

"*No!*" said Robert, with indignation.

"Well, then!" said the Phoenix. "And as to the rain—
well, I am not fond of rain myself. If the sun knew *I* was
here—he's very fond of shining on me because I look so
bright and golden. He always says I repay a little attention.
Haven't you some form of words suitable for use in wet
weather?"

"There's 'Rain, rain, go away,' " said Anthea. "But it never *does* go."

"Perhaps you don't say the invocation properly," said the bird.

> "Rain rain, go away,
> Come again another day
> Little baby wants to play,"

said Anthea.

"That's quite wrong; and if you say it in that sort of dull way, I can quite understand the rain not taking any notice. You should open the window and shout as loud as you can:

> 'Rain, rain, go away,
> Come again another day;
> Now we want the sun, and so,
> Pretty rain, be kind and go!'

You should always speak politely to people when you want them to do things, and especially when it's going away that you want them to do. And today you might add:

> 'Shine, great sun, the lovely Phoe-
> Nix is here, and wants to be
> Shone on, splendid sun, by thee!'

"That's poetry!" said Cyril decidedly.

"It's like it," said the more cautious Robert.

"I was obliged to put in 'lovely,' " said the Phoenix modestly, "to make the line long enough."

"There are plenty of nasty words just that length," said Jane, but everyone else said "Hush!"

And then they opened the window and shouted the seven lines as loud as they could, and the Phoenix said all the words with them, except "lovely," and when they came to that it looked down and coughed bashfully.

The rain hesitated a moment and then went away.

"There's true politeness," said the Phoenix, and the next moment it was perched on the window ledge, opening and shutting its radiant wings and flapping out its golden feathers in such a flood of glorious sunshine as you sometimes have at sunset in autumn time. People said afterward that there had not been such sunshine in December for years and years and years.

"And now," said the bird, "we will go out into the city, and you shall take me to see one of my temples."

"Your temples?"

"I gather from the carpet that I have many temples in this land."

"I don't see how you *can* find anything out from it," said Jane. "It never speaks."

"All the same, you can pick up things from a carpet," said the bird. "I've seen *you* do it. And I have picked up several pieces of information in this way. That papyrus on which you showed me my picture—I understand that it bears on it the name of the street of your city in which my finest temple stands, with my image graved in stone and in metal over against its portal."

"You mean the fire insurance office," said Robert. "It's not really a temple, and they don't—"

"Excuse me," said the Phoenix coldly, "you are wholly misinformed. It *is* a temple, and they do."

"Don't let's waste the sunshine," said Anthea. "We might argue as we go along, to save time."

So the Phoenix consented to make itself a nest in the breast of Robert's Norfolk jacket, and they all went out into the splendid sunshine. The best way to the temple of the Phoenix seemed to be to take the tram, and on the top of it the children talked, while the Phoenix now and then put out a wary beak, cocked a cautious eye, and contradicted what the children were saying.

It was a delicious ride, and the children felt how lucky they were to have had the money to pay for it. They went with the tram as far as it went, and when it did not go any farther they stopped too, and got off. The tram stops at the end of the Gray's Inn Road, and it was Cyril who thought that one might well find a shortcut to the Phoenix Office through the little streets and courts that lie tightly packed between Fetter Lane and Ludgate Circus. Of course, he was quite mistaken, as Robert told him at the time, and afterward Robert did not forbear to remind his brother how he had said so. The streets there were small and stuffy and ugly, and crowded with printers' boys and binders' girls coming out from work; and these stared so hard at the pretty red coats and caps of the sisters that they wished they had gone some other way. And the printers and binders made very personal remarks, advising Jane to get her hair cut and inquiring where Anthea had bought that hat. Jane and Anthea scorned to reply, and Cyril and Robert found that they were hardly a match for the rough crowd. They could think of nothing nasty enough to say. They turned a corner sharply, and then Anthea pulled Jane into an archway, and then inside a door;

Cyril and Robert quickly followed, and the jeering crowd passed by without seeing them.

Anthea drew a long breath.

"How awful!" she said. "I didn't know there were such people, except in books."

"It was a bit thick; but it's partly you girls' fault, coming out in those flashy coats."

"We thought we ought to, when we were going out with the Phoenix," said Jane; and the bird said, "Quite right too"—and incautiously put out his head to give her a wink of encouragement. And at the same instant a dirty hand reached through the grim balustrade of the staircase beside them and clutched the Phoenix, and a hoarse voice said:

"I say, Urb, blowed if this ain't our Poll parrot what we lost. Thank you very much, lidy, for bringin' 'im home to roost."

The four turned swiftly. Two large and ragged boys were crouched amid the dark shadows of the stairs. They were much larger than Robert and Cyril, and one of them had snatched the Phoenix away and was holding it high above their heads.

"Give me that bird," said Cyril sternly. "It's ours."

"Good arternoon, and thankin' you," the boy went on with maddening mockery. "Sorry I can't give yer tuppence for yer trouble—but I've 'ad to spend my fortune advertising for my vallyable bird in all the newspapers. You can call for the reward next year."

"Look out, Ike," said his friend a little anxiously. "It 'ave a beak on it."

"It's other parties as'll have the Beak on to 'em presently," said Ike darkly, "if they come a-trying to lay claims on my

Poll parrot. You just shut up, Urb. Now, then, you four little gells, get our er this."

"Little girls!" cried Robert. "I'll little girl you!" He sprang up three stairs and hit out.

There was a squawk—the most birdlike noise anyone had every heard from the Phoenix—and a fluttering, and a laugh in the darkness, and Ike said:

"There now, you've been and gone and strook my Poll parrot right in the fevvers—strook 'im something crool, you 'ave."

Robert stamped with fury. Cyril felt himself growing pale with rage and with the effort of screwing up his brain to make it clever enough to think of some way of being even with those boys. Anthea and Jane were as angry as the boys, but it made them want to cry. Yet it was Anthea who said:

"Do, *please*, let us have the bird."

"Dew, *please*, get along and leave us an' our bird alone."

"If you don't," said Anthea, "I shall fetch the police."

"You better!" said he who was named Urb. "Say, Ike, you twist the bloomin' pigeon's neck; he ain't wuth tuppence."

"Oh, no," cried Jane, "don't hurt it. Oh, don't; it is such a pet."

"I won't hurt it," said Ike. "I'm 'shamed of you, Urb, for to think of such a thing. Arf a shiner, miss, and the bird is yours for life."

"Half a *what?*" asked Anthea.

"Arf a shiner, quid, thick 'un—half a sov, then."

"I haven't got it—and, besides, it's *our* bird," said Anthea.

"Oh, don't talk to him," said Cyril; and then Jane said suddenly:

"Phoenix—dear Phoenix, we can't do anything. *You* must manage it."

"With pleasure," said the Phoenix—and Ike nearly dropped it in his amazement.

"I say, it do talk, suthin' like," said he.

"Youths," said the Phoenix, "sons of misfortune, hear my words."

"My eyes!" said Ike.

"Look out, Ike," said Urb, "you'll throttle the joker—and I see at wunst 'e wuth 'is weight in flimsies."

"Hearken, O Eikonoclastes, despiser of sacred images—and thou, Urbanus, dweller in the sordid city. Forbear this adventure lest a worse thing befall."

"Luv' us!" said Ike. "Ain't it been taught its schoolin', just!"

"Restore me to my young acolytes and escape unscathed. Retain me—and—"

"They must ha' got all this up, case the Polly got pinched," said Ike. "Lor' lumme, the artfulness of them young 'uns!"

"I say, slosh 'em in the geseech and get clear off with the swag's wot I say," urged Herbert.

"Right-o," said Isaac.

"Forbear," repeated the Phoenix sternly. "Who pinched the click off of the old bloke in Aldermanbury?" it added in a changed tone. "Who sneaked the nose rag out of the young gell's 'and in Bell Court? Who—"

"Stow it," said Ike. "You! ugh! yah!—leave go of me. Bash him off, Urb, 'e'll 'ave my bloomin' eyes outer my 'ed."

There were howls, a scuffle, a flutter; Ike and Urb fled up the stairs, and the Phoenix swept out through the doorway. The children followed and the Phoenix settled on Robert, "like a butterfly on a rose," as Anthea said afterward, and wriggled into the breast of his Norfolk jacket, "like an eel into mud," as Cyril later said.

"Why ever didn't you burn him? You could have, couldn't you?" asked Robert, when the hurried flight through the narrow courts had ended in the safe wideness of Farringdon Street.

"I could have, of course," said the bird, "but I didn't think it would be dignified to allow myself to get warm about a little thing like that. The Fates, after all, have not been illiberal to me. I have a good many friends among the London sparrows, and I have a beak and claws."

These happenings had somewhat shaken the adventurous temper of the children, and the Phoenix had to exert its golden self to hearten them up.

Presently the children came to a great house in Lombard Street, and there, on each side of the door, was the image of the Phoenix carved in stone, and set forth on shining brass were the words:

PHOENIX FIRE OFFICE

"One moment," said the bird. "Fire? For altars, I suppose?"

"*I* don't know," said Robert; he was beginning to feel shy, and that always made him rather cross.

"Oh, yes, you do," Cyril contradicted. "When people's houses are burnt down the Phoenix gives them new houses. Father told me; I asked him."

"The house, then, like the Phoenix, rises from its ashes? Well have my priests dealt with the sons of men!"

"The sons of men pay, you know," said Anthea, "but it's only a little every year."

"That is to maintain my priests," said the bird, "who, in the hour of affliction, heal sorrows and rebuild houses. Lead on; inquire for the High Priest. I will not break upon them too suddenly in all my glory. Noble and honor-deserving are they who make as nought the evil deeds of the lame-footed and unpleasing Hephaestus."

"I don't know what you're talking about, and I wish you wouldn't muddle us with new names. Fire just happens. Nobody does it—not as a deed, you know," Cyril explained. "If they did, the Phoenix wouldn't help them, because it's a crime to set fire to things. Arsenic, or something, they call it, because it's as bad as poisoning people. The Phoenix wouldn't help *them*—Father told me it wouldn't."

"My priests do well," said the Phoenix. "Lead on."

"I don't know what to say," said Cyril; and the others said the same.

"Ask for the High Priest," said the Phoenix. "Say that you have a secret to unfold that concerns my worship, and he will lead you to the innermost sanctuary."

So the children went in, all four of them, though they didn't like it, and stood in a large and beautiful hall adorned with Doulton tiles, like a large and beautiful bath with no water in it, and stately pillars supporting the roof. An unpleasing representation of the Phoenix in brown pottery disfigured one wall. There were counters and desks of mahogany and brass, and clerks bent over the desks and walked behind the counters. There was a great clock over an inner doorway.

"Inquire for the High Priest," whispered the Phoenix.

An attentive clerk in decent black, who controlled his mouth but not his eyebrows, now came toward them. He leaned forward on the counter, and the children thought he was going to say, "What can I have the pleasure of showing you?" like in a draper's; instead of which the young man said:

"And what do *you* want?"

"We want to see the High Priest."

"Get along with you," said the young man.

An elder man, also decent in black coat, advanced.

"Perhaps it's Mr. Blank" (not for worlds would I give the name). "He's a Masonic High Priest, you know."

A porter was sent away to look for Mr. Asterisk (I cannot give his name), and the children were left there to look on and be looked on by all the gentlemen at the mahogany desks. Anthea and Jane thought that they looked kind. The boys thought they stared, and that it was like their cheek.

The porter returned with the news that Mr. Dot Dash Dot (I dare not reveal his name) was out, but that Mr.——

Here a really delightful gentleman appeared. He had a beard and a kind and merry eye, and each one of the four knew at once that this was a man who had kiddies of his own and could understand what you were talking about. Yet it was a difficult thing to explain.

"What is it?" he asked. "Mr.——"— he named the name which I will never reveal—"is out. Can I do anything?"

"Inner sanctuary," murmured the Phoenix.

"I beg your pardon," said the nice gentleman, who thought it was Robert who had spoken.

"We have something to tell you," said Cyril, "but"—he glanced at the porter, who was lingering much nearer than he need have done—"this is a very public place."

The nice gentleman laughed.

"Come upstairs, then," he said, and led the way up a wide and beautiful staircase. Anthea says the stairs were of white marble, but I am not sure. On the corner post of the stairs, at the top, was a beautiful image of the Phoenix in dark metal, and on the wall at each side was a flat sort of image of it.

The nice gentleman led them into a room where the chairs, and even the tables, were covered with reddish leather. He looked at the children inquiringly.

"Don't be frightened," he said. "Tell me exactly what you want."

"May I shut the door?" asked Cyril.

The gentleman looked surprised, but he shut the door.

"Now," said Cyril firmly. "I know you'll be awfully surprised, and you'll think it's not true and we are lunatics; but we aren't and it is. Robert's got something inside his Norfolk— that's Robert, he's my young brother. Now don't be upset and have a fit or anything, sir. Of course, I know when you called your shop the 'Phoenix' you never thought there was one; but there is—and Robert's got it buttoned up against his chest!"

"If it's an old curio in the form of a Phoenix, I daresay the Board—" said the nice gentleman as Robert began to fumble with his buttons.

"It's old enough," said Anthea, "going by what it says, but—"

"My goodness gracious!" said the gentleman, as the Phoenix, with one last wriggle that melted into a flutter, got out of its nest in the breast of Robert and stood up on the leather-covered table.

"What an extraordinarily fine bird!" he went on. "I don't think I ever saw one just like it."

"I should think not," said the Phoenix with pardonable pride. And the gentleman jumped.

"Oh, it's been taught to speak! Some sort of parrot, perhaps?"

"I am," said the bird simply, "the Head of your House, and I have come to my temple to receive your homage. I am no parrot"—its beak curved scornfully—"I am the one and only Phoenix, and I demand the homage of my High Priest."

"In the absence of our manager—" the gentleman began, exactly as though he were addressing a valued customer, "in the absence of our manager, I might perhaps be able— What am I saying?" He turned pale and passed his hand across his brow. "My dears," he said, "the weather is unusually warm for the time of year, and I don't feel quite myself. Do you know, for a moment I really thought that that remarkable bird of yours had spoken and said it was the Phoenix, and, what's more, that I'd believed it."

"So it did, sir," said Cyril, "and so did you."

"It really— Allow me."

A bell was rung. The porter appeared.

"Mackenzie," said the gentleman, "you see that golden bird?"

"Yes, sir."

The other breathed a sigh of relief.

"It *is* real, then?"

"Yes, sir, of course, sir. You take it in your hand, sir," said the porter sympathetically, and reached out his hand to the Phoenix, who shrank back on toes curved with agitated indignation.

"Forbear!" it cried. "How dare you seek to lay hands on me?"

The porter saluted.

"Beg pardon, sir," he said, "I thought you was a bird."

"I *am* a bird—*the* bird—the Phoenix."

"Of course you are, sir," said the porter. "I see that the first minute, directly I got my breath, sir."

"That will do," said the gentleman. "Ask Mr. Wilson and Mr. Sterry to step up here for a moment, please."

Mr. Sterry and Mr. Wilson were in their turn overcome by amazement—quickly followed by conviction. To the surprise of the children, everyone in the office took the Phoenix at its word, and after the first shock of surprise it seemed to be perfectly natural to everyone that the Phoenix should be alive, and that, passing through London, should call at its temple.

"We ought to have some sort of ceremony," said the nicest gentleman anxiously. "There isn't time to summon the directors and shareholders—we might do that tomorrow, perhaps. Yes, the boardroom would be best. I shouldn't like it to feel we hadn't done everything in our power to show our appreciation of its condescension in looking in on us in this friendly way."

The children could hardly believe their ears, for they had never thought that anyone but themselves would believe in the Phoenix. And yet everyone did; all the men in the office were brought in by twos and threes, and the moment the Phoenix opened its beak it convinced the cleverest of them, as well as those who were not so clever. Cyril wondered how the story would look in the papers next day.

He seemed to see the posters in the streets:

PHOENIX FIRE OFFICE
THE PHOENIX AT ITS TEMPLE
MEETING TO WELCOME IT
DELIGHT OF THE MANAGER AND EVERYBODY

"Excuse our leaving you a moment," said the nice gentleman, and he went away with the others; and through the
half-closed door the children could hear the sound of many
boots on stairs, the hum of excited voices explaining, sug-
gesting, arguing, the thumpy drag of heavy furniture being
moved about.

The Phoenix strutted up and down the leather-covered
table, looking over its shoulder at its pretty back.

"You see what a convincing manner I have," it said
proudly.

And now a new gentleman came in and said, bowing low:

"Everything is prepared—we have done our best at so
short a notice; the meeting—the ceremony—will be in the
boardroom. Will the Honorable Phoenix walk—it is only a
few steps—or would it like to be—would it like some sort of
conveyance?"

"My Robert will bear me to the boardroom, if that be the
unlovely name of my temple's inmost court," replied the bird.

So they all followed the gentleman. There was a big table
in the boardroom, but it had been pushed right up under the
long windows at one side, and chairs were arranged in rows
across the room—like those you have at schools when there
is a magic lantern* on Our Eastern Empire, or on The Way

---

*Slide show

We Do in the Navy. The doors were of carved wood, very beautiful, with a carved Phoenix above. Anthea noticed that the chairs in the front rows were of the kind that her mother so loved to ask the price of in old furniture shops, and never could buy, because the price was always nearly twenty pounds each. On the mantelpiece were some heavy bronze candlesticks and a clock, and on the top of the clock was another image of the Phoenix.

"Remove that effigy," said the Phoenix to the gentlemen who were there, and it was hastily taken down. Then the Phoenix fluttered to the middle of the mantelpiece and stood there, looking more golden than ever. Then everyone in the house and the office came in—from the cashier to the women who cooked the clerks' dinners in the beautiful kitchen at the top of the house. And everyone bowed to the Phoenix and then sat down in a chair.

"Gentlemen," said the nicest gentleman, "we have met here today—"

The Phoenix was turning its golden beak from side to side.

"I don't notice any incense," it said, with an injured sniff.

A hurried consultation ended in plates being fetched from the kitchen. Brown sugar, sealing wax, and tobacco were placed on these, and something from a square bottle was poured over it all. Then a match was applied. It was the only incense that was handy in the Phoenix office, and it certainly burned very briskly and smoked a great deal.

"We have met here today," said the gentleman again, "on an occasion unparalleled in the annals of this office. Our respected Phoenix—"

"Head of the House," said the Phoenix in a hollow voice.

"I was coming to that. Our respected Phoenix, the Head

of this ancient House, has at length done us the honor to come among us. I think I may say, gentlemen, that we are not insensible to this honor, and that we welcome with no uncertain voice one whom we have so long desired to see in our midst."

Several of the younger clerks thought of saying "Hear, hear," but they feared it might seem disrespectful to the bird.

"I will not take up your time," the speaker went on, "by recapitulating the advantages to be derived from a proper use of our system of fire insurance. I know, and you know, gentlemen, that our aim has ever been to be worthy of that eminent bird whose name we bear and who now adorns our mantelpiece with his presence. Three cheers, gentlemen, for the winged Head of the House!"

The cheers rose, deafening. When they had died away the Phoenix was asked to say a few words.

It expressed in graceful phrases the pleasure it felt in finding itself at last in its own temple.

"And," it went on, "you must not think me wanting in appreciation of your hearty and cordial reception when I ask that an ode may be recited or a choric song sung. It is what I have always been accustomed to."

The four children, dumb witnesses of this wonderful scene, glanced a little nervously across the foam of white faces above the sea of black coats. It seemed to them that the Phoenix was really asking a little too much.

"Time presses," said the Phoenix, "and the original ode of invocation is long, as well as being Greek; and, besides, it's no use invoking me when here I am; but is there not a song in your own tongue for a great day such as this?"

Absently the manager began to sing, and one by one the rest joined:

> "Absolute security!
> No liability!
> All kinds of property
> Insured against fire.
> Terms most favorable,
> Expenses reasonable,
> Moderate rates for annual
>      Insurance. . . ."

"That one is *not* my favorite," interrupted the Phoenix, "and I think you've forgotten part of it."

The manager hastily began another.

> "O Golden Phoenix, fairest bird,
> The whole great world has often heard
> Of all the splendid things we do,
> Great Phoenix, just to honor you."

"That's better," said the bird.
And everyone sang:

> "Class one, for private dwelling house,
> For household goods and shops allows;
> Provided these are built of brick
> Or stone, and tiled and slated thick."

"Try another verse," said the Phoenix, "further on."
And again arose the voices of all the clerks and employees and managers and secretaries and cooks:

"In Scotland our insurance yields
The price of burnt-up stacks in fields."

"Skip that verse," said the Phoenix.

"Thatched dwellings and their whole contents
We deal with—also with their rents;
Oh, glorious Phoenix, look and see
That these are dealt with in class three.

"The glories of your temple throng
Too thick to go in any song;
And we attend, O, good and wise,
To 'days of grace' and merchandise.

"When people's homes are burned away
They never have a cent to pay
If they have done as all should do,
O Phoenix, and have honored you.

"So let us raise our voice and sing
The praises of the Phoenix King.
In classes one and two and three,
Oh, trust to him, for kind is he!"

"I'm sure *you're* very kind," said the Phoenix. "And now we must be going. And thank you very much for a very pleasant time. May you all prosper as you deserve to do, for I am sure a nicer, pleasanter-spoken lot of temple attendants I have never met, and never wish to meet. I wish you all good day!"

It fluttered to the wrist of Robert and drew the four children from the room. The whole of the office staff followed down the wide stairs and filed into their accustomed places, and the two most important officials stood on the steps bowing till Robert had buttoned the golden bird in his Norfolk bosom, and it and he and the three other children were lost in the crowd.

The two most important gentlemen looked at each other earnestly and strangely for a moment, and then retreated to those sacred inner rooms, where they toil without ceasing for the good of the House.

And the moment they were all in their places—managers, secretaries, clerks, and porters—they all started, and each looked cautiously round to see if anyone was looking at him. For each thought that he had fallen asleep for a few minutes, and had dreamed a very odd dream about the Phoenix and the boardroom. And, of course, no one mentioned it to anyone else, because going to sleep at your office is a thing you simply *must not* do.

The extraordinary confusion of the boardroom, with the remains of the incense in the plates, would have shown them at once that the visit of the Phoenix had been no dream but a radiant reality, but no one went into the boardroom again that day; and next day, before the office was opened, it was all cleaned and put nice and tidy by a lady whose business asking questions was not part of. That is why Cyril read the papers in vain on the next day and the day after that; because no sensible person thinks his dreams worth putting in the paper, and no one will ever own that he has been asleep in the daytime.

The Phoenix was very pleased, but it decided to write an

ode for itself. It thought the ones it had heard at its temple had been too hastily composed. Its own ode began:

> For beauty and for modest worth
> The Phoenix has not its equal on earth.

And when the children went to bed that night it was still trying to cut down the last line to the proper length without taking out any of what it wanted to say.

That is what makes poetry so difficult.

# Chapter 6

# Doing Good

"**W**e shan't be able to go anywhere on the carpet for a whole week, though," said Robert.

"And I'm glad of it," said Jane unexpectedly.

"Glad?" said Cyril. "*Glad?*"

It was breakfasttime, and Mother's letter, telling them how they were all going for Christmas to their aunt's at Lyndhurst and how Father and Mother would meet them there, having been read by everyone, lay on the table, drinking hot bacon fat with one corner and eating marmalade with the other.

"Yes, glad," said Jane. "I don't want any more things to happen just now. I feel like you do when you've been to three parties in a week—like we did at Granny's once—and extras in between, toys and chocs and things like that. I want everything to be just real, and no fancy things happening at all."

"I don't like being obliged to keep things from Mother," said Anthea. "I don't know why, but it makes me feel selfish and mean."

"If we could only get the mater to believe it, we might

take her to the jolliest places," said Cyril thoughtfully. "As it is, we've just *got* to be selfish and mean—if it is that—but I don't feel it is."

"I *know* it isn't, but I *feel* it is," said Anthea, "and that's just as bad."

"It's worse," said Robert. "If you knew it and didn't feel it it wouldn't matter so much."

"That's being an hardened criminal, Father says," put in Cyril, and he picked up Mother's letter and wiped its corners with his handkerchief, to whose color a trifle of bacon fat and marmalade made but little difference.

"We're going tomorrow, anyhow," said Robert. "Don't," he added, with a good-boy expression on his face, "don't let's be ungrateful for our blessings; don't let's waste the day in saying how horrid it is to keep secrets from mothers, when we all know Anthea tried all she knew to give her the secret, and she wouldn't take it. You'll have time enough to repent of things all next week."

"Yes," said Cyril, "let's. It's not really wrong."

"Well, look here," said Anthea. "You know there's something about Christmas that makes you want to be good—however little you wish it at other times. Couldn't we wish the carpet to take us somewhere where we should have the chance to do some good and kind action? It would be an adventure just the same," she pleaded.

"I don't mind," said Cyril. "We shan't know where we're going, and that'll be exciting. No one knows what'll happen. We'd best put on our outers, in case—"

"We might rescue a traveler buried in the snow, like St. Bernard dogs, with barrels round our necks," said Jane, beginning to be interested.

"Or we might arrive just in time to witness a will being signed—more tea, please," said Robert, "and we should see the old man hide it away in the secret cupboard; and then, after long years, when the rightful heir was in despair, we should lead him to the hidden panel and—"

"Yes," interrupted Anthea. "Or we might be taken to some freezing garret in a German town, where a poor little pale, sick child—"

"We haven't any German money," interrupted Cyril, "so *that's* no go. What I should like would be getting into the middle of a war and getting hold of secret intelligence and taking it to the general, and he would make me a lieutenant, or a scout, or a hussar."

When breakfast was cleared away Anthea swept the carpet and the children sat down on it, together with the Phoenix, who had been specially invited, as a Christmas treat, to come with them and witness the good and kind action they were about to do.

Four children and one bird were ready, and the wish was wished.

Everyone closed its eyes, so as to feel the topsy-turvy swirl of the carpet's movement as little as possible.

When the eyes were opened again the children found themselves on the carpet, and the carpet was in its proper place on the floor of their own nursery at Camden Town.

"I say," said Cyril, "here's a go!"

"Do you think it's worn out? The wishing part of it, I mean?" Robert anxiously asked the Phoenix.

"It's not that," said the Phoenix, "but—well—what did you wish?"

"Oh! I see what it means," said Robert with deep disgust.

"It's like the end of a fairy story in a Sunday magazine. How perfectly beastly!"

"You mean it means we can do kind and good actions where we are? I see. I suppose it wants us to carry coals for the cook or make clothes for the bare heathens. Well, I simply won't. And the last day and everything. Look here!" Cyril spoke loudly and firmly. "We want to go somewhere really interesting, where we have a chance of doing something good and kind; we don't want to do it here, but somewhere else. See? Now, then."

The obedient carpet started instantly, and the four children and one bird fell in a heap together, and as they fell were plunged in perfect darkness.

"Are you all there?" said Anthea breathlessly, through the black dark. Everyone owned that it was there.

"Where are we? Oh! how shivery and wet it is! Ugh! Oh! I've put my hand in a puddle!"

"Has anyone got any matches?" said Anthea hopelessly. She felt sure that no one would have any.

It was then that Robert, with a radiant smile of triumph that was quite wasted in the darkness, where, of course, no one could see anything, drew out of his pocket a box of matches, struck a match, and lighted a candle—two candles. And everyone, with its mouth open, blinked at the sudden light.

"Well done, Bobs," said his sisters, and even Cyril's natural brotherly feelings could not check his admiration of Robert's foresight.

"I've always carried them about since the lone tower day," said Robert with modest pride. "I knew we should want them someday. I kept the secret well, didn't I?"

"Oh, yes," said Cyril with fine scorn. "I found them the Sunday after, when I was feeling in your Norfolk for the knife you borrowed off me. But I thought you'd only sneaked them for Chinese lanterns, or reading in bed by."

"Bobs," said Anthea suddenly, "do you know where we are? This is *the* underground passage, and look there—there's the money and the moneybags, and everything."

By this time the ten eyes had got used to the light of the candles, and no one could help seeing that Anthea spoke the truth.

"It seems an odd place to do good and kind acts in, though," said Jane. "There's no one to do them to."

"Don't you be too sure," said Cyril. "Just round the next turning we might find a prisoner who has languished here for years and years, and we could take him out on our carpet and restore him to his sorrowing friends."

"Of course we could," said Robert, standing up and holding the candle above his head to see farther off. "Or we might find the bones of a poor prisoner and take them to his friends to be buried properly—that's always a kind action in books, though I never could see what bones matter."

"I wish you wouldn't," said Jane.

"I know exactly where we shall find the bones too," Robert went on. "You see that dark arch just along the passage? Well, just inside there—"

"If you don't stop going on like that," said Jane firmly, "I shall scream and then I'll faint—so now then!"

"And *I* will too," said Anthea.

Robert was not pleased at being checked in his flight of fancy.

"You girls will never be great writers," he said bitterly.

"They just love to think of things in dungeons, and chains and knobbly bare human bones, and—"

Jane had opened her mouth to scream, but before she could decide how you began when you wanted to faint the golden voice of the Phoenix spoke through the gloom.

"Peace!" it said. "There are no bones here except the small but useful sets that you have inside you. And you did not invite me to come out with you to hear you talk about bones, but to see you do some good and kind action."

"We can't do it here," said Robert sulkily.

"No," rejoined the bird. "The only thing we can do here, it seems, is to try to frighten our little sisters."

"He didn't, really, and I'm not so *very* little," said Jane, rather ungratefully.

Robert was silent. It was Cyril who suggested that perhaps they had better take the money and go.

"That wouldn't be a kind act, except to ourselves; and it wouldn't be good, whatever way you look at it," said Anthea, "to take money that's not ours."

"We might take it and spend it all on benefits to the poor and aged," said Cyril.

"That wouldn't make it right to steal," said Anthea stoutly.

"I don't know," said Cyril. They were all standing up now. "Stealing is taking things that belong to someone else, and there's no one else."

"It can't be stealing if—"

"That's right," said Robert with ironical approval. "Stand here all day arguing while the candles burn out. You'll like it awfully when it's all dark again—and bony."

"Let's get out, then," said Anthea. "We can argue as we go." So they rolled up the carpet and went. But when they had crept along to the place where the passage led into the topless tower, they found the way blocked by a great stone, which they could not move.

"There!" said Robert. "I hope you're satisfied!"

"Everything has two ends," said the Phoenix softly. "Even a quarrel or a secret passage."

So they turned round and went back, and Robert was made to go first with one of the candles, because he was the one who had begun to talk about bones. And Cyril carried the carpet.

"I wish you hadn't put the bones into our heads," said Jane as they went along.

"I didn't; you always had them. More bones than brains," said Robert.

The passage was long, and there were arches and steps and turnings and dark alcoves that the girls did not much like passing. The passage ended in a flight of steps. Robert went up them.

Suddenly he staggered heavily back on to the following feet of Jane, and everybody screamed, "Oh! What is it?"

"I've only bashed my head in," said Robert, when he had groaned for some time. "That's all. Don't mention it; I like it. The stairs just go right slap into the ceiling, and it's a stone ceiling. You can't do good and kind actions underneath a paving stone."

"Stairs aren't made to lead you just to paving stones as a general rule," said the Phoenix. "Put your shoulder to the wheel."

"There isn't any wheel," said the injured Robert, still rubbing his head.

But Cyril had pushed past him to the top stair and was

already shoving his hardest against the stone above. Of course, it did not give in the least.

"If it's a trapdoor—" said Cyril. And he stopped shoving and began to feel about with his hands. "Yes, there *is* a bolt. I can't move it."

By a happy chance Cyril had in his pocket the oil can of his father's bicycle; he put the carpet down at the foot of the stairs, and he lay on his back, with his head on the top step and his feet straggling down among his young relations, and he oiled the bolt till the drops of rust and oil fell down on his face. One even went into his mouth—open, as he panted with exertion of keeping up this unnatural position. Then he tried again, but still the bolt would not move. So now he tied his handkerchief—the one with the bacon fat and marmalade on it—to the bolt, and Robert's handkerchief to that, in a reef knot, which cannot come undone however much you pull and, indeed, gets tighter and tighter the more you pull it. This must not be confused with a granny knot, which comes undone if you look at it. And then he and Robert pulled, and the girls put their arms around their brothers and pulled too, and suddenly the bolt gave way with a rusty scrunch, and they all rolled together to the bottom of the stairs—all but the Phoenix, which had taken to its wings when the pulling began.

Nobody was hurt much, because the rolled-up carpet broke their fall; and now, indeed, the shoulders of the boys were used to some purpose, for the stone allowed them to heave it up. They felt it give; dust fell freely on them.

"Now, then," cried Robert, forgetting his head and his temper, "push all together. One, two, three!"

The stone was heaved up. It swung up on a creaking,

unwilling hinge, and showed a growing oblong of dazzling daylight; and it fell back with a bang against something that kept it upright. Everyone climbed out, but there was not room for everyone to stand comfortably in the little paved house where they found themselves, so when the Phoenix had fluttered up from the darkness they let the stone down and it closed like a trapdoor, as indeed it was.

You can have no idea how dusty and dirty the children were. Fortunately there was no one to see them but each other. The place they were in was a little shrine, built on the side of the road that went winding up through yellow-green fields to the topless tower. Below them were fields and orchards, all bare boughs and brown furrows, and little houses and gardens. The shrine was a kind of tiny chapel with no front wall—just a place for people to stop and rest in and wish to be good. So the Phoenix told them. There was an image that had once been brightly colored, but the rain and snow had beaten in through the open front of the shrine, and the poor image was dull and weather-stained. Under it was written: *"St. Jean de Luz. Priez pour nous."* It was a sad little place, very neglected and lonely, and yet it was nice, Anthea thought, that poor travelers should come to this little resthouse in the hurry and worry of their journeyings and be quiet for a few minutes, and think about being good. The thought of St. Jean de Luz—who had, no doubt, in his time been very good and kind—made Anthea want more than ever to do something kind and good.

"Tell us," she said to the Phoenix, "what is the good and kind action the carpet brought us here to do?"

"I think it would be kind to find the owners of the treasure and tell them about it," said Cyril.

"And give it them *all?*" said Jane.

"Yes. But whose is it?"

"I should go to the first house and ask the name of the owner of the castle," said the golden bird, and really the idea seemed a good one.

They dusted each other as well as they could and went down the road. A little way on they found a tiny spring, bubbling out of the hillside and falling into a rough stone basin surrounded by draggled hart's tongue ferns, now hardly green at all. Here the children washed their hands and faces and dried them on their pocket handkerchiefs, which always, on these occasions, seem unnaturally small. Cyril's and Robert's handkerchiefs, indeed, rather undid the effects of the wash. But in spite of this the party certainly looked cleaner than before.

The first house they came to was a little white house with green shutters and a slate roof. It stood in a prim little garden, and down each side of the neat path were large stone vases for flowers to grow in; but all the flowers were dead now.

Along one side of the house was a sort of wide verandah, built of poles and trellis-work, and a vine crawled all over it. It was wider than our English verandahs, and Anthea thought it must look lovely when the green leaves and the grapes were there; but now there were only dry, reddish-brown stalks and stems, with a few withered leaves caught in them.

The children walked up to the front door. It was green and narrow. A chain with a handle hung beside it and joined itself quite openly to a rusty bell that hung under the porch. Cyril had pulled the bell and its noisy clang was dying away before the terrible thought came to all. Cyril spoke it.

"My hat!" he breathed. "We don't know any French!"

At this moment the door opened. A very tall, lean lady, with pale ringlets like whitey-brown paper or oak shavings, stood before them. She had an ugly gray dress and a black silk apron. Her eyes were small and gray and not pretty, and the rims were red, as though she had been crying.

She addressed the party in something that sounded like a foreign language, and ended with something which they were sure was a question. Of course, no one could answer it.

"What does she say?" Robert asked, looking down into the hollow of his jacket, where the Phoenix was nestling. But before the Phoenix could answer the whitey-brown lady's face was lighted up by a most charming smile.

"You—you ar-r-re fr-r-rom the England!" she cried. "I love so much the England. *Mais entrez—entrez donc tous!* Enter, then—enter all. One essuyes his feet on the carpet."

She pointed to the mat.

"We only wanted to ask—"

"I shall say you all that what you wish," said the lady. "Enter only!"

So they all went in, wiping their feet on a very clean mat, and putting the carpet in a safe corner of the verandah.

"The most beautiful days of my life," said the lady, as she shut the door, "did pass themselves in England. And since long time I have not heard an English voice to repeal me the past."

This warm welcome embarrassed everyone, but most the boys, for the floor of the hall was of such very clean red and white tiles, and the floor of the sitting room so very shiny—like a black looking glass—that each felt as though he had on far more boots than usual, and far noisier.

There was a wood fire, very small and very bright, on the hearth—neat little logs laid on brass fire dogs. Some portraits of powdered ladies and gentlemen hung in oval frames on the pale walls. There were silver candlesticks on the mantelpiece, and there were chairs and a table, very slim and polite, with slender legs. The room was extremely bare, but with a bright foreign bareness that was very cheerful, in an odd way of its own.

At the end of the polished table a very un-English little boy sat on a footstool in a high-backed, uncomfortable-looking chair. He wore black velvet, and the kind of collar—all frills and lacey—that Robert would rather have died than wear; but then the little French boy was much younger than Robert.

"Oh, how pretty!" said everyone. But no one meant the little French boy, with the velvety short knickerbockers and the velvety short hair.

What everyone admired was a little, little Christmas tree, very green, and standing in a very red little flowerpot, and hung round with very bright little things made of tinsel and colored paper. There were tiny candles on the tree, but they were not lighted yet.

"But yes—is it not that it is genteel?" said the lady. "Sit down you then, and let us see."

The children sat down in a row on the stiff chairs against the wall, and the lady lighted a long, slim red taper at the wood flame, and then she drew the curtains and lit the little candles, and when they were all lighted the little French boy suddenly shouted, "Bravo, *ma tante! Oh, que c'est gentil,*" and the English children shouted, "Hooray!"

Then there was a struggle in the breast of Robert, and out

fluttered the Phoenix—spread his gold wings, flew to the top of the Christmas tree, and perched there.

"Ah! catch it, then," cried the lady. "It will itself burn—your genteel parrakeet!"

"It won't," said Robert, "thank you."

And the little French boy clapped his clean and tidy hands; but the lady was so anxious that the Phoenix fluttered down and walked up and down on the shiny walnut-wood table.

"Is it that it talks?" asked the lady.

And the Phoenix replied in excellent French. It said, *"Parfaitement, madame!"*

"Oh, the pretty parrakeet," said the lady. "Can it say still of other things?"

And the Phoenix replied, this time in English, "Why are you sad so near Christmastime?"

The children looked at it and with one gasp of horror and surprise, for the youngest of them knew that it is far from manners to notice that strangers have been crying, and much worse to ask them the reason of their tears. And, of course, the lady began to cry again, very much indeed, after calling the Phoenix a bird without a heart; and she could not find her handkerchief, so Anthea offered hers, which was still very damp and no use at all. She also hugged the lady, and this seemed to be of more use than the handkerchief, so that presently the lady stopped crying and found her own handkerchief and dried her eyes, and called Anthea a cherished angel.

"I am sorry we came just when you were so sad," said Anthea, "but we really only wanted to ask you whose that castle is on the hill."

"Oh, my little angel," said the poor lady, sniffing, "today

and for hundreds of years the castle is to us, to our family. Tomorrow it must that I sell it—to some strangers—and my little Henri, who ignores all, he will not have never the lands paternal. But what will you? His father, my brother—Mr. the Marquis—has spent much of money, and it the must, despite the sentiments of familial respect, that I admit that my sainted father he also—"

"How would you feel if you found a lot of money—hundreds and thousands of gold pieces?" asked Cyril.

The lady smiled sadly.

"Ah! One has already recounted to you the legend?" she said. "It is true that one says that it is long time; oh! but long time, one of our ancestors has hid a treasure—of gold, and of gold, and of gold—enough to enrich my little Henri for the life. But all that, my children, it is but the accounts of fays—"

"She means fairy stories," whispered the Phoenix to Robert. "Tell her what you have found."

So Robert told, while Anthea and Jane hugged the lady for fear she should faint for joy, like people in books, and they hugged her with the earnest, joyous hugs of unselfish delight.

"It's no use explaining how we got in," said Robert, when he had told of the finding of the treasure, "because you would find it a little difficult to understand, and much more difficult to believe. But we can show you where the gold is and help you to fetch it away."

The lady looked doubtfully at Robert as she absently returned the hugs of the girls.

"No, he's not making it up," said Anthea. "It's true, *true*, TRUE!—and we *are* so glad."

"You would not be capable to torment an old woman?" she said. "And it is not possible that it be a dream."

"It really *is* true," said Cyril, "and I congratulate you very much."

His tone of studied politeness seemed to convince more than the raptures of the others.

"If I do not dream," she said, "Henri come to Manon—and you—you shall come all with me to Mr. the Curate. Is it not?"

Manon was a wrinkled old woman with a red and yellow handkerchief twisted round her head. She took Henri, who was already sleepy with the excitement of his Christmastree and his visitors, and when the lady had put on a stiff black cape and a wonderful black silk bonnet and a pair of black wooden clogs over her black cashmere house boots, the whole party went down the road to a little white house—very like the one they had left—where an old priest, with a good face, welcomed them with a politeness so great that it hid his astonishment.

The lady, with her French waving hands and her shrugging French shoulders and her trembling French speech, told the story. And now the priest, who knew no English, shrugged *his* shoulders and waved *his* hands and spoke also in French.

"He thinks," whispered the Phoenix, "that her troubles have turned her brain. What a pity you know no French!"

"I do know a lot of French," whispered Robert indignantly, "but it's all about the pencil of the gardener's son and the penknife of the baker's niece—nothing that anyone ever wants to say."

"If *I* speak," the bird whispered, "he'll think *he's* mad too."

"Tell me what to say."

"Say '*C'est vrai, monsieur. Venez donc voir,*' " said the Phoenix; and then Robert earned the undying respect of everybody by suddenly saying, very loudly and distinctly:

"Say vray, mossoo; venny dong vwaw."

The priest was disappointed when he found that Robert's French began and ended with these useful words, but, at any rate, he saw that if the lady was mad she was not the only one, and he put on a big beavery hat, and got a candle and matches and a spade, and they all went up the hill to the wayside shrine of St. John of Luz.

"Now," said Robert, "I will go first and show you where it is."

So they prised the stone up with a corner of the spade, and Robert did go first, and they all followed and found the golden treasure exactly as they had left it. And everyone was flushed with the joy of performing such a wonderfully kind action.

Then the lady and the priest clasped hands and wept for joy, as French people do, and knelt down and touched the money, and talked very fast and both together, and the lady embraced all the children three times each, and called them "little garden angels," and then she and the priest shook each other by both hands again, and talked, and talked, and talked, faster and more Frenchy than you would have believed possible. And the children were struck dumb with joy and pleasure.

"Get away *now*," said the Phoenix softly, breaking in on the radiant dream.

So the children crept away, and out through the little shrine, and the lady and the priest were so tearfully, talkatively happy that they never noticed that the guardian angels had gone.

The "garden angels" ran down the hill to the lady's little house, where they had left the carpet in the verandah, and they spread it out and said, "Home," and no one saw them disappear, except little Henri, who had flattened his nose into a white button against the window glass, and when he tried to tell his aunt she thought he had been dreaming. So that was all right.

"It is much the best thing we've done," said Anthea, when they talked it over at teatime. "In the future we'll only do kind actions with the carpet."

"Ahem!" said the Phoenix.

"I beg your pardon?" said Anthea.

"Oh, nothing," said the bird. "I was only thinking!"

# Chapter 7

# Mews from Persia

**W**hen you hear that the four children found themselves at Waterloo Station quite un-taken-care-of, and with no one to meet them, it may make you think that their parents were neither kind nor careful. But if you think this you will be wrong. The fact is, Mother arranged with Aunt Emma that she was to meet the children at Waterloo, when they went back from their Christmas holiday at Lyndhurst. The train was fixed, but not the day. Then Mother wrote to Aunt Emma, giving her careful instructions about the day and the hour, and about luggage and cabs and things, and gave the letter to Robert to post. But the hounds happened to meet near Rufus Stone that morning, and what is more, on the way to the meet they met Robert, and Robert met them, and instantly forgot all about posting Aunt Emma's letter, and never thought of it again until he and the others had wandered three times up and down the platform at Waterloo—which makes six in all—and had bumped against old gentlemen, and stared in the faces of ladies, and been shoved by people in a hurry, and "by-your-leaved" by porters with trucks, and were quite, quite sure that Aunt Emma was not there.

Then suddenly the true truth of what he had forgotten to do came home to Robert, and he said, "Oh, crikey!" and stood still with his mouth open, and let a porter with a Gladstone bag in each hand and a bundle of umbrellas under one arm blunder heavily into him, and never so much as said "Where are you shoving to now?" or "Look out where you're going, can't you?" The heavier bag smote him at the knee, and he staggered, but he said nothing.

When the others understood what was the matter I think they told Robert what they thought of him.

"We must take the train to Croydon," said Anthea, "and find Aunt Emma."

"Yes," said Cyril, "and precious pleased those Jevonses would be to see us and our traps."*

Aunt Emma, indeed, was staying with some Jevonses— very prim people. They were middle-aged and wore very smart blouses, and they were fond of matinees and shopping, and they did not care about children.

"I know *Mother* would be pleased to see us if we went back," said Jane.

"Yes, she would, but she'd think it was not right to show she was pleased, because it's Bob's fault we're not met. Don't I know the sort of thing?" said Cyril. "Besides, we've no tin. No; we've got enough for a growler among us, but not enough for tickets to the New Forest. We must just go home. They won't be so savage when they find we've really got

---

*Carriages

home all right. You know auntie was only going to take us home in a cab."

"I believe we ought to go to Croydon," Anthea insisted.

"Aunt Emma would be out to a dead cert," said Robert. "Those Jevonses go to the theater every afternoon, I believe. Besides, there's the Phoenix at home, *and* the carpet. I votes we call a four-wheeled cabman."

A four-wheeled cabman was called—his cab was one of the old-fashioned kind with straw in the bottom—and he was asked by Anthea to drive them very carefully to their address. This he did, and the price he asked for doing so was exactly the value of the gold coin Grandpapa had given Cyril for Christmas. This cast a gloom; but Cyril would never have stooped to argue about a cabfare, for fear the cabman should think he was not accustomed to take cabs whenever he wanted them. For a reason that was something like this he told the cabman to put the luggage on the steps, and waited till the wheels of the growler had grittily retired before he rang the bell.

"You see," he said, with his hand on the handle, "we don't want Cook and Eliza asking us before *him* how it is we've come home alone, as if we were babies."

Here he rang the bell; and the moment its answering clang was heard, everyone felt that it would be some time before that bell was answered. The sound of the bell is quite different, somehow, when there is anyone inside the house who hears it. I can't tell you why that is—but so it is.

"I expect they're changing their dresses," said Jane.

"Too late," said Anthea, "it must be past five. I expect Eliza's gone to post a letter, and Cook's gone to see the time."

Cyril rang again. And the bell did its best to inform the listening children that there was really no one human in the house. They rang again and listened intently. The hearts of all sank low. It is a terrible thing to be locked out of your own house, on a dark, muggy January evening.

"There is no gas on anywhere," said Jane, in a broken voice.

"I expect they've left the gas on once too often, and the draught blew it out, and they're suffocated in their beds. Father always said they would someday," said Robert cheerfully.

"Let's go and fetch a policeman," said Anthea, trembling.

"And be taken up for trying to be burglars—no, thank you," said Cyril. "I heard Father read out of the paper about a young man who got into his own mother's house, and they got him made a burglar only the other day."

"I only hope the gas hasn't hurt the Phoenix," said Anthea. "It *said* it wanted to stay in the bathroom cupboard, and I thought it would be all right, because the servants *never* clean that out. But if it's gone and got out and been choked by gas— And besides, directly we open the door we shall be choked too. I *knew* we ought to have gone to Aunt Emma at Croydon. Oh, Squirrel, I wish we had. Let's go *now*."

"Shut up," said her brother briefly. "There's someone rattling the latch inside."

Everyone listened with all its ears, and everyone stood back as far from the door as the steps would allow.

The latch rattled, and clicked. Then the flap of the letter box lifted itself—everyone saw it by the flickering light of the gas lamp that shone through the leafless lime tree by the gate—a golden eye seemed to wink at them through the letter slit, and a cautious beak whispered:

"Are you alone?"

"It's the Phoenix," said everyone, in a voice so joyous, and so full of relief, as to be a sort of whispered shout.

"Hush!" said the voice form the letter-box slit. "Your slaves have gone a-merry-making. The latch of this portal is too stiff for my beak. But at the side—the little window above the shelf whereon your bread lies—it is not fastened."

"Righto!" said Cyril.

And Anthea added, "I wish you'd meet us there, dear Phoenix."

The children crept round to the pantry window. It is at the side of the house, and there is a green gate labeled "Tradesmen's Entrance," which is always kept bolted. But if you get one foot on the fence between you and next door, and one on the handle of the gate, you are over before you know where you are. This, at least, was the experience of Cyril and Robert, and even, if the truth must be told, of Anthea and Jane. So in almost no time all four were in the narrow graveled passage that runs between that house and the next.

Then Robert made a back, and Cyril hoisted himself up and got his knickerbockered knee on the concrete window-sill. He dived into the pantry head first, as one dives into water, and his legs waved in the air as he went, just as your legs do when you are first beginning to learn to dive. The soles of his boots—squarish muddy patches—disappeared.

"Give me a leg up," said Robert to his sisters.

"No, you don't," said Jane firmly. "I'm not going to be left outside here with just Anthea, and have something creep up behind us out of the dark. Squirrel can go and open the back door."

A light had sprung awake in the pantry. Cyril always said the Phoenix turned the gas on with its beak, and lighted it with a waft of his wing, but he was excited at the time, and perhaps he really did it himself with matches, and then forgot all about it. He let the others in by the back door. And when it had been bolted again the children went all over the house and lighted every single gas jet they could find. For they couldn't help feeling that this was just the dark dreary winter's evening when an armed burglar might easily be expected to appear at any moment. There is nothing like light when you are afraid of burglars—or of anything else, for that matter.

And when all the gas jets were lighted it was quite clear that the Phoenix had made no mistake, and that Eliza and Cook were really out, and that there was no one in the house except the four children, and the Phoenix, and the carpet, and the blackbeetles who lived in the cupboards on each side of the nursery fireplace. These last were very pleased that the children had come home again, especially when Anthea had lighted the nursery fire. But, as usual, the children treated the loving little blackbeetles with coldness and disdain.

I wonder whether you know how to light a fire? I don't mean how to strike a match and set fire to the corners of the paper in a fire someone else has laid ready, but how to lay and light a fire all by yourself. I will tell you how Anthea did it, and if ever you have to light one yourself you may remember how it is done. First, she raked out the ashes of the fire that had burned there a week ago—for Eliza had actually never done this, though she had had plenty of time. In doing this Anthea knocked her knuckle and made it bleed.

Then she laid the largest and handsomest cinders in the bottom of the grate. Then she took a sheet of old newspaper (you ought never to light a fire with today's newspaper—it will not burn well, and there are other reasons against it), and tore it into four quarters, and screwed each of these into a loose ball, and put them on the cinders; then she got a bundle of wood and broke the string, and stuck the sticks in so that their front ends rested on the bars, and the back end on the back of the paper balls. In doing this she cut her finger slightly with the string, and when she broke it two of the sticks jumped up and hit her on the cheek. Then she put more cinders and some bits of coal—no dust. She put most of that on her hands, but there seemed to be enough left for her face. Then she lighted the edges of the paper balls, and waited till she heard the fizz-crack-crack-fizz of the wood as it began to burn. Then she went and washed her hands and face under the tap in the back kitchen.

Of course, you need not bark your knuckles, or cut your finger, or bruise your cheek with wood, or black yourself all over; but otherwise, this is a very good way to light a fire in London. In the real country fires are lighted in a different and prettier way. But it is always good to wash your hands and face afterward, wherever you are.

While Anthea was delighting the poor little blackbeetles with the cheerful blaze, Jane had set the table for—I was going to say tea, but the meal of which I am speaking was not exactly tea. Let us call it a teaish meal. There was tea, certainly, for Anthea's fire blazed and crackled so kindly that it really seemed to be affectionately inviting the kettle to come and sit upon its lap. So the kettle was brought and tea made. But no milk could be found—so everyone had six lumps of sugar to each cup instead. The things to eat, on the other hand, were nicer than usual. The boys looked about very carefully, and found in the pantry some cold tongue, bread, butter, cheese, and part of a cold pudding—very much nicer than Cook ever made when they were at home. And in the kitchen cupboard was half a Christmassy cake, a pot of strawberry jam, and about a pound of mixed candied fruit, with soft crumbly slabs of delicious sugar in each cup of lemon, orange, or citron.

It was indeed, as Jane said, "a banquet fit for an Arabian knight."

The Phoenix perched on Robert's chair, and listened kindly and politely to all they had to tell it about their visit to Lyndhurst, and underneath the table, by just stretching a toe down rather far, the faithful carpet could be felt by all—even by Jane, whose legs were very short.

"Your slaves will not return tonight," said the Phoenix. "They sleep under the roof of the cook's stepmother's aunt, who is, I gather, hostess to a large party tonight in honor of her husband's cousin's sister-in-law's mother's ninetieth birthday."

"I don't think they ought to have gone without leave," said Anthea, "however many relations they have, or however old they are. But I suppose we ought to wash up."

"It's not our business about the leave," said Cyril firmly, "but I simply won't wash up for them. We got it, and we'll clear it away; and then we'll go somewhere on the carpet. It's not often we get a chance of being out all night. We can go right away to the other side of the equator, to the tropical climes, and see the sun rise over the great Pacific Ocean."

"Right you are," said Robert. "I always did want to see the Southern Cross and the stars as big as gas lamps."

"*Don't* go," said Anthea very earnestly, "because I *couldn't.* I'm *sure* Mother wouldn't like us to leave the house, and I should hate to be left here alone."

"I'd stay with you," said Jane loyally.

"I know you would," said Anthea gratefully, "but even with you I'd much rather not."

"Well," said Cyril, trying to be kind and amiable. "I don't want you to do anything you think's wrong, *but—*"

He was silent; this silence said many things.

"I don't see—" Robert was beginning, when Anthea interrupted.

"I'm quite sure. Sometimes you just think a thing's wrong, and sometimes you *know.* And this is a *know* time."

The Phoenix turned kind golden eyes on her and opened a friendly beak to say:

"When it is, as you say, a 'know time,' there is no more to be said. And your noble brothers would never leave you."

"Of course not," said Cyril rather quickly. And Robert said so too.

"I myself," the Phoenix went on, "am willing to help in any way possible. I will go personally—either by carpet or on the wing—and fetch you anything you can think of to amuse you during the evening. In order to waste no time I could go while you wash up. Why," it went on in a musing voice, "does one wash up teacups and wash down the stairs?"

"You couldn't wash stairs up, you know," said Anthea, "unless you began at the bottom and went up feet first as you washed. I wish Cook would try that for a change."

"I don't," said Cyril briefly. "I should hate the look on her elastic-side boots sticking up."

"This is mere trifling," said the Phoenix. "Come, decide what I shall fetch for you. I can get you anything you like."

But of course they couldn't decide. Many things were suggested—a rocking horse, jeweled chessmen, an elephant, a bicycle, a motorcar, books with pictures, musical instruments, and many other things. But a musical instrument is agreeable only to the player, unless he has learned to play it really well; books are not sociable, bicycles cannot be ridden without going out of doors, and the same is true of motor cars and elephants. Only two people can play chess at once with one set of chessmen (and anyway it's very much too much like lessons for a game), and only one can ride on a rocking horse. Suddenly, in the midst of the discussion, the Phoenix spread its wings and fluttered to the floor, and from there it spoke.

"I gather," it said, "from the carpet that it wants you to let it go to its old home, where it was born and brought up, and it will return within the hour laden with a number of the most beautiful and delightful products of its native land."

"What is its native land?"

"I didn't gather. But since you can't agree, and time is passing, and the tea things are not washed down—I mean washed up—"

"I votes we do," said Robert. "It'll stop all this jaw, anyway. And it's not bad to have surprises. Perhaps it's a Turkey carpet, and it might bring us Turkish delight."

"Or Turkish patrol," said Robert.

"Or a Turkish bath," said Anthea.

"Or a Turkish towel," said Jane.

"Nonsense," Robert urged, "it said beautiful and delightful, and towels and baths aren't *that*, however good they may
be for you. Let it go. I suppose it won't give us the slip," he
added, pushing back his chair and standing up.

"Hush!" said the Phoenix. "How can you? Don't trample
on its feelings just because it's only a carpet."

"But how can it do it—unless one of us is on it to do the
wishing?" asked Robert. He spoke with a rising hope that it
*might* be necessary for one to go—and why not Robert? But
the Phoenix quickly threw cold water on his newborn dream.

"Why, you just write your wish on a paper, and pin it on
the carpet."

So a leaf was torn from Anthea's arithmetic book, and on
it Cyril wrote in large round-hand the following:

> We wish you to go to your dear native home,
> and bring back the most beautiful and delightful
> productions of it you can—and not to be gone long,
> please.
>
> (Signed) Cyril.<br>Robert.<br>Anthea.<br>Jane.

Then the paper was laid on the carpet.

"Writing down, please," said the Phoenix. "The carpet
can't read a paper whose back is turned to it, any more than
you can."

It was pinned fast, and the table and chairs having been
moved, the carpet simply and suddenly vanished, rather
like a patch of water on a hearth under a fierce fire. The

edges got smaller and smaller, and then it disappeared from sight.

"It may take it some time to collect the beautiful and delightful things," said the Phoenix. "I should wash up—I mean wash down."

So they did. There was plenty of hot water left in the kettle, and everyone helped—even the Phoenix, who took up cups by their handles with its clever claws and dipped them in the hot water, and then stood them on the table ready for Anthea to dry them. But the bird was rather slow, because, as it said, though it was not above any sort of honest work, messing about with dishwater was not exactly what it had been brought up to. Everything was nicely washed up, and dried, and put in its proper place, and the dishcloth washed and hung on the edge of the copper to dry, and the tea cloth was hung on the line that goes across the scullery. (If you are a duchess's child, or a king's, or a person of high social position's child, you will perhaps not know the difference between a dishcloth and a tea cloth; but in that case your nurse has been better instructed than you; and she will tell you all about it.) And just as eight hands and one pair of claws were being dried on the roller towel behind the scullery door, there came a strange sound from the other side of the kitchen wall—the side where the nursery was. It was a very strange sound, indeed—most odd, and unlike any other sounds the children had ever heard. At least, they had heard sounds as much like it as a toy engine's whistle is like a steam siren's.

"The carpet's come back," said Robert; and the others felt that he was right.

"But what has it brought with it?" asked Jane. "It sounds like Leviathan, that great beast—"

"It couldn't have been made in India, and have brought elephants? Even baby ones would be rather awful in that room," said Cyril. "I vote we take it in turns to squint through the keyhole."

They did—in the order of their ages. The Phoenix, being the eldest by some thousands of years, was entitled to the first peep. But:

"Excuse me," it said, ruffling its golden feathers and sneezing softly. "Looking through keyholes always gives me a cold in my golden eyes."

So Cyril looked.

"I see something gray moving," said he.

"It's a zoological garden of some sort, I bet," said Robert, when he had taken his turn. And the soft rustling, bustling, ruffling, scuffling, shuffling, fluffling, noise went on inside.

"I can't see anything," said Anthea, "my eye tickles so."

Then Jane's turn came, and she put her eye to the keyhole.

"It's a giant kitty cat," she said, "and it's asleep all over the floor."

"Giant cats are tigers—Father said so."

"No, he didn't. He said tigers were giant cats. It's not at all the same thing."

"It's no use sending the carpet to fetch precious things for you if you're afraid to look at them when they come," said the Phoenix sensibly.

And Cyril, being the eldest, said, "Come on," and turned the handle.

The gas had been left full on after tea, and everything in the room could be plainly seen by the ten eyes at the door. At least, not everything, for though the carpet was there, it was invisible, because it was completely covered by the hundred and ninety-nine beautiful objects which it had brought from its birthplace.

"My hat!" Cyril remarked. "I never thought about its being a *Persian* carpet."

Yet it was now plain that it was so, for the beautiful objects which it had brought back were cats—Persian cats, gray Persian cats, and there were, as I have said, one hundred and ninety-nine of them, and they were sitting on the carpet as close as they could get to each other. But the moment the children entered the room the cats rose and stretched, and spread and overflowed from the carpet to the floor, and in an instant the floor was a sea of moving mewing pussishness, and the children with one accord climbed to the table, and gathered up their legs, and the people next door knocked on the wall—and, indeed, no wonder, for the mews were Persian and piercing.

"This is pretty poor sport," said Cyril. "What's the matter with the bounders?"

"I imagine that they are hungry," said the Phoenix. "If you were to feed them—"

"We haven't anything to feed them with," said Anthea in despair, and she stroked the nearest Persian back. "Oh, pussies, do be quiet—we can't hear ourselves think."

She had to shout this entreaty, for the mews were growing deafening. "And it would take pounds and pounds worth of cat's meat."

"Let's ask the carpet to take them away," said Robert.

But the girls said "No."

"They are so soft and pussy," said Jane.

"And valuable," said Anthea hastily. "We can sell them for lots and lots of money."

"Why not send the carpet to get food for them?" suggested the Phoenix, and its golden voice became harsh and cracked with the effort it had to make to be heard above the increasing fierceness of the Persian mews.

So it was written that the carpet should bring food for one hundred and ninety-nine Persian cats, and the paper was pinned to the carpet as before.

The carpet seemed to gather itself together, and the cats dropped off it, as raindrops do from your mackintosh when you shake it. And the carpet disappeared.

Unless you have had one hundred and ninety-nine well-grown Persian cats in one small room, all hungry, and all saying so in unmistakable mews, you can form but a poor idea of the noise that now deafened the children and the Phoenix. The cats did not seem to have been at all properly brought up. They seemed to have no idea of its being a mistake in manners to ask for meals in a strange house—let alone to howl for them—and they mewed, and they mewed, and they mewed, and they mewed, till the children poked their fingers into their ears and waited in silent agony, wondering why the whole of Camden Town did not come knocking at the door to ask what was the matter, and only hoping that the food for the cats would come before the neighbors did—and before all the secret of the carpet and the Phoenix had to be given away beyond recall to an indignant neighborhood.

The cats mewed and mewed and twisted their Persian forms in and out and unfolded their Persian tails, and the children and the Phoenix huddled together on the table.

The Phoenix, Robert noticed suddenly, was trembling.

"So many cats," it said, "and they might not know I was the Phoenix. These accidents happen so quickly. It quite unmans me."

This was a danger of which the children had not thought. "Creep in," cried Robert, opening his jacket.

And the Phoenix crept in—only just in time, for green eyes had glared, pink noses had sniffed, white whiskers had twitched, and as Robert buttoned his coat he disappeared to the waist in a wave of eager gray Persian fur. And on the instant the good carpet slapped itself down on the floor. And it was covered with rats—three hundred and ninety-eight of them, I believe, two for each cat.

"How horrible!" cried Anthea. "Oh, take them away!"

"Take yourself away," said the Phoenix, "and me."

"I wish we'd never had a carpet," said Anthea, in tears.

They hustled and crowded out of the door, and shut it, and locked it. Cyril, with great presence of mind, lit a candle and turned off the gas at the main.

"The rats'll have a better chance in the dark," he said.

The mewing had ceased. Everyone listened in breathless silence. We all know that cats eat rats—it is one of the first things we read in our little brown reading books; but all those cats eating all those rats—it wouldn't bear thinking of.

Suddenly Robert sniffed, in the silence of the dark kitchen, where the only candle was burning all on one side, because of the draught.

"What a funny scent!" he said.

And as he spoke, a lantern flashed its light through the windows of the kitchen, a face peered in, and a voice said:

"What's all this row about? You let me in."

It was the voice of the police!

Robert tiptoed to the window and spoke through the pane that had been a little cracked since Cyril accidentally knocked it with a walking stick when he was playing at balancing it on his nose. (It was after they had been to a circus.)

"What do you mean?" he said. "There's no row. You listen; everything's as quiet as quiet."

And indeed it was.

The strange sweet scent grew stronger, and the Phoenix put out its beak.

The policeman hesitated.

"They're *mus*krats," said the Phoenix. "I suppose some cats eat them—but never Persian ones. What a mistake for a well-informed carpet to make! Oh, what a night we're having!"

"Do go away," said Robert nervously. "We're just going to bed—that's our bedroom candle; there isn't any row. Everything's as quiet as a mouse."

A wild chorus of mews drowned his words, and with the mews were mingled the shrieks of the muskrats. What had happened? Had the cats tasted them before deciding that they disliked the flavor?

"I'm a-coming in," said the policeman. "You've got a cat shut up there."

"A cat," said Cyril. "Oh, my only aunt! A cat!"

"Come in, then," said Robert. "It's your own lookout. I advise you not. Wait a shake, and I'll undo the side gate."

He undid the side gate, and the policeman, very cautiously, came in.

And there in the kitchen, by the light of one candle, with the mewing and the screaming going on like a dozen steam sirens, twenty waiting motor cars, and half a hundred squeaking pumps, four agitated voices shouted to the policeman four mixed and wholly different explanations of the very mixed events of the evening.

Did you ever try to explain the simplest thing to a policeman?

# Chapter 8

# The Cats, the Cow, and the Burglar

*T*he nursery was full of Persian cats and muskrats that had been brought there by the wishing carpet. The cats were mewing and the muskrats were squeaking so that you could hardly hear yourself speak. In the kitchen were the four children, one candle, a concealed Phoenix, and a very visible policeman.

"Now then, look here," said the policeman very loudly, and he pointed his lantern at each child in turn. "What's the meaning of this here yelling and caterwauling? I tell you you've got a cat here, and someone's a ill-treating of it. What do you mean by it, eh?"

It was five to one, counting the Phoenix; but the policeman, who was one, was of unusually fine size, and the five, including the Phoenix, were small. The mews and the squeaks grew softer, and in the comparative silence Cyril said:

"It's true. There are a few cats here. But we've not hurt them. It's quite the opposite. We've just fed them."

"It don't sound like it," said the policeman grimly.

"I daresay they're not *real* cats," said Jane madly. "Perhaps they're only dream cats."

"I'll dream cat you, my lady," was the brief response of the force.

"If you understood anything except people who do murders and stealings and naughty things like that, I'd tell you all about it," said Robert, "but I'm certain you don't. You're not meant to shove your oar into people's private cat-keepings. You're only supposed to interfere when people shout 'murder' and 'stop thief' in the street. So there."

The policeman assured them that he should see about that, and at this point the Phoenix, who had been making himself small on the pot shelf under the dresser, among the saucepan lids and the fish kettle, walked on tiptoed claws in a noiseless and modest manner and left the room unnoticed by anyone.

"Oh, don't be so horrid," Anthea was saying, gently and earnestly. "We *love* cats—dear pussy-soft things. We wouldn't hurt them for worlds. Would we, Pussy?"

And Jane answered that of course they wouldn't. And still the policeman seemed unmoved by their eloquence.

"Now, look here," he said, "I'm a-goin' to see what's in that room beyond there, and—"

His voice was drowned in a wild burst of mewing and squeaking. And as soon as it died down all four children began to explain at once; and though the squeaking and mewing were not at their very loudest, yet there was quite enough of both to make it very hard for the policeman to understand a single word of any of the four wholly different explanations now poured out to him.

"Stow it," he said at last. "I'm a-goin' into the next room in the execution of my duty. I'm a-goin' to use my eyes—my ears have gone off their chumps, what with you and them cats."

And he pushed Robert aside and strode through the door.

"Don't say I didn't warn you," said Robert.

"It's tigers *really*," said Jane. "Father said so. I wouldn't go in, if I were you."

But the policeman was quite stony; nothing anyone said seemed to make any difference to him. Some policemen are like this, I believe. He strode down the passage, and in another moment he would have been in the room with all the cats and all the rats (musk), but at that very instant a thin, sharp voice screamed from the street outside:

"Murder—murder! Stop thief!"

The policeman stopped, with one regulation boot heavily poised in the air.

"Eh?" he said.

And again the shrieks sounded shrilly and piercingly from the dark street outside.

"Come on," said Robert. "Come and look after cats while somebody's being killed outside." For Robert had an inside feeling that told him quite plainly *who* it was that was screaming.

"You young rip," said the policeman, "I'll settle up with you bimeby."

And he rushed out, and the children heard his boots going weightily along the pavement, and the screams also going along, rather ahead of the policeman; and both the murder screams and the policeman's boots faded away in the remote distance.

Then Robert smacked his knickerbocker loudly with his palm, and said:

"Good old Phoenix! I should know its golden voice anywhere."

And then everyone understood how cleverly the Phoenix had caught at what Robert had said about the real work of a policeman being to look after murderers and thieves, and not after cats, and all hearts were filled with admiring affection.

"But he'll come back," said Anthea mournfully, "as soon as he finds the murderer is only a bright vision of a dream, and there isn't one at all really."

"No, he won't," said the soft voice of the clever Phoenix, as it flew in. *"He does not know where your house is. I heard him own as much to a fellow mercenary. Oh! what a night we are having! Lock the door, and let us rid ourselves of this intolerable smell of the perfume peculiar to the muskrat and to the house of the trimmers of beards. If you'll excuse me, I will go to bed. I am worn out."*

It was Cyril who wrote the paper that told the carpet to take away the rats and bring milk, because there seemed to be no doubt in any breast that, however Persian cats may be, they must have milk.

"Let's hope it won't be muskmilk," said Anthea, in gloom, as she pinned the paper face-downward on the carpet. "Is there such a thing as a musk cow?" she added anxiously, as the carpet shriveled and vanished. "I do hope not. Perhaps really it *would* have been wiser to let the carpet take the cats away. It's getting quite late, and we can't keep them all night."

"Oh, can't we?" was the bitter rejoinder of Robert, who had been fastening the side door. "You might have consulted me," he went on. "I'm not such an idiot as some people."

"Why, whatever—"

"Don't you see? We've jolly well *got* to keep the cats all night—oh, get down, you furry beasts!—because we've had three wishes out of the old carpet now, and we can't get any more till tomorrow."

The liveliness of Persian mews alone prevented the occurrence of a dismal silence.

Anthea spoke first.

"Never mind," she said. "Do you know, I really do think they're quieting down a bit. Perhaps they heard us say milk."

"They can't understand English," said Jane. "You forget they're Persian cats, Panther."

"Well," said Anthea rather sharply, for she was tired and anxious, "who told you milk wasn't Persian for milk? Lots of English words are just the same in French—at least, I know "miaw" is, and "croquet," and "fiancé." Oh, pussies, do be quiet! Let's stroke them as hard as we can with both hands, and perhaps they'll stop."

So everyone stroked gray fur till their hands were tired and as soon as a cat had been stroked enough to make it stop mewing it was pushed gently away, and another mewing mouser was approached by the hands of the strokers. And the noise was really more than half purr when the carpet suddenly appeared in its proper place, and on it, instead of rows of milk cans, or even of milk jugs, there was a *cow*. Not a Persian cow either, nor, most fortunately, a musk cow, if there is such a thing, but a smooth, sleek, dun-colored Jersey cow, who blinked large soft eyes at the gaslight and mooed in an amiable if rather inquiring manner.

Anthea had always been afraid of cows; but now she tried to be brave.

"Anyway, it can't run after me," she said to herself. "There isn't room for it even to begin to run."

The cow was perfectly placid. She behaved like a strayed duchess till someone brought a saucer for the milk and someone else tried to milk the cow into it. Milking is very difficult. You may think it is easy, but it is not. All the children were by this time strung up to a pitch of heroism that would have been impossible to them in their ordinary condition. Robert and Cyril held the cow by the horns; and Jane, when she was quite sure that their end of the cow was quite secure, consented to stand by, ready to hold the cow by the tail should occasion arise. Anthea, holding the saucer, now advanced toward the cow. She remembered to have heard that cows, when milked by strangers, are susceptible to the soothing influence of the human voice. So, clutching her saucer very tight, she sought for words to whose soothing influence the cow might be susceptible. And her memory, troubled by the events of the night, which seemed to go on and on forever and ever, refused to help her with any form of words suitable to address a Jersey cow in.

"Poor pussy, then. Lie down, then, good dog, lie down!" was all that she could think to say, and she said it.

And nobody laughed. The situation, full of gray mewing cats, was too serious for that.

Then Anthea, with a beating heart, tried to milk the cow. Next moment the cow had knocked the saucer out of her hand and trampled on it with one foot, while with the other three she had walked on a foot each of Robert, Cyril, and Jane.

Jane burst into tears.

"Oh, how much too horrid everything is!" she cried.

"Come away. Let's go to bed and leave the horrid cats with the hateful cow. Perhaps somebody will eat somebody else. And serve them right."

They did not go to bed, but they had a shivering council in the drawing room, which smelt of soot—and, indeed, a heap of this lay in the fender. There had been no fire in the room since Mother went away, and all the chairs and tables were in the wrong places, and the chrysanthemums were dead and the water in the pot nearly dried up. Anthea wrapped the embroidered woolly sofa blanket round Jane and herself, while Robert and Cyril had a struggle, silent and brief, but fierce, for the larger share of the fur hearthrug.

"It is mostly truly awful," said Anthea, "and I *am* so tired. Let's let the cats loose."

"And the cow, perhaps?" said Cyril. "The police would find us at once. That cow would stand at the gate and mew—I mean moo—to come in. And so would the cats. No; I see quite well what we've got to do. We must put them in baskets and leave them on people's doorsteps, like orphan foundlings."

"We've got three baskets, counting Mother's work one," said Jane, brightening.

"And there are nearly two hundred cats," said Anthea, "besides the cow—and it would have to be a different-sized basket for her; and then I don't know how you'd carry it, and you'd never find a doorstep big enough to put it on. Except the church one, and—"

"Oh, well," said Cyril, "if you simply *make* difficulties—"

"I'm with you," said Robert. "Don't fuss about the cow, Panther. It's simply *got* to stay the night, and I'm sure I've read that the cow is a remunerating creature, and that means it will sit still and think for hours. The carpet can take it away in the morning. And as for the baskets, we'll do them in dusters, or pillowcases, or bath towels. Come on, Squirrel. You girls can be out of it if you like."

His tone was full of contempt, but Jane and Anthea were too tired and desperate to care; even being "out of it," which at other times they could not have borne, now seemed quite a comfort. They snugged down in the sofa blanket, and Cyril threw the fur hearthrug over them.

"Ah," he said, "that's all women are fit for—to keep safe and warm while the men do the work and run dangers and risks and things."

"I'm not," said Anthea. "You know I'm not."

But Cyril was gone.

It was warm under the blanket and the hearthrug, and Jane snugged up close to her sister; and Anthea cuddled Jane closely and kindly, and in a sort of dream they heard the rise of a wave of mewing as Robert opened the door of the nursery. They heard the booted search for baskets in the back kitchen. They heard the side door open and close, and they knew that each brother had gone out with at least one cat. Anthea's last thought was that it would take at least all night to get rid of one hundred and ninety-nine cats by twos. There would be ninety-nine journeys of two cats each, and one cat over.

"I almost think we might keep the one cat over," said Anthea. "I don't seem to care for cats just now, but I daresay I shall again someday." And she fell asleep. Jane also was sleeping.

It was Jane who awoke with a start, to find Anthea still asleep. As in the act of awakening, she kicked her sister, she

wondered idly why they should have gone to bed in their
boots; but the next moment she remembered where they
were.

There was a sound of muffled, shuffled feet on the stairs.
Like the heroine of the classic poem, Jane "thought it was the
boys," and as she felt quite wide awake and not nearly so
tired as before, she crept gently from Anthea's side and
followed the footsteps. They went down into the basement;
the cats, who seemed to have fallen into the sleep of exhaus-
tion, awoke at the sound of the approaching footsteps and
mewed piteously. Jane was at the foot of the stairs before she
saw it was not her brothers whose coming had roused her and
the cats, but a burglar. She knew he was a burglar at once
because he wore a fur cap and a red and black charity-check
comforter and he had no business where he was.

If you had stood in Jane's shoes you would no doubt have
run away in them, appealing to the police and neighbors
with horrid screams. But Jane knew better. She had read a
great many nice stories about burglars, as well as some affecting pieces of poetry, and she knew that no burglar will ever
hurt a little girl if he meets her when burgling. Indeed, in all
the cases Jane had read of, his burglarishness was almost at
once forgotten in the interest he felt in the little girl's artless
prattle. So if Jane hesitated for a moment before addressing
the burglar, it was only because she could not at once think
of any remark sufficiently prattling and artless to make a
beginning with. In the stories and the affecting poetry the
child could never speak plainly, though it always looked old
enough to in the pictures. And Jane could not make up her
mind to lisp and "talk baby," even to a burglar. And while
she hesitated he softly opened the nursery door and went in.

Jane followed—just in time to see him sit down flat on the floor, scattering cats as a stone thrown into a pool splashes water.

She closed the door softly and stood there, still wondering whether she *could* bring herself to say "What's 'oo doing here, Mithter Wobber?" and whether any other kind of talk would do.

Then she heard the burglar draw a long breath, and he spoke:

"It's a judgment," he said, "so help me bob if it ain't. Oh, 'ere's a thing to 'appen to a chap! Make it come 'ome to you, don't it neither? Cats an' cats an' cats. There couldn't be all them cats. Let alone the cow. If she ain't the moral of the old man's Daisy. She's a dream out of when I was a lad—I don't mind 'er so much. 'Eree, Daisy, Daisy?"

The cow turned and looked at him.

"*She's* all right," he went on. "Sort of company too. Though them above knows how she got into this downstairs parlor. But them cats—oh, take 'em away, take 'em away! I'll chuck the 'ole show—oh, take 'em away."

"Burglar," said Jane, close behind him, and he started convulsively, and turned on her a blank face, whose pale lips trembled. "I can't take those cats away."

"Lor' lumme!" exclaimed the man. "If 'ere ain't another on 'em. Are you real, miss, or something I'll wake up from presently?"

"I am quite real," said Jane, relieved to find that a lisp was not needed to make the burglar understand her. "And so," she added, "are the cats."

"Then send for the police, send for the police, and I'll go quiet. If you ain't no realer than them cats, I'm done, spunchuck—out of time. Send for the police. I'll go quiet. One thing, there'd not be room for 'arf them cats in no cell as ever I see."

He ran his fingers through his hair, which was short, and his eyes wandered wildly round the room full of cats.

"Burglar," said Jane, kindly and softly, "if you didn't like cats, what did you come here for?"

"Send for the police," was the unfortunate criminal's only reply. "I'd rather you wouldn't—honest, I'd rather."

"I daren't," said Jane, "and besides I've no one to send. I hate the police. I wish he'd never been born."

"You've a feeling 'art, miss," said the burglar, "but them cats is really a little bit too thick."

"Look here," said Jane, "I won't call the police. And I am quite a real little girl, though I talk older than the kind you've met before when you've been doing your burglings. And they *are* real cats—and they want real milk—and— Didn't you say the cow was like somebody's Daisy that you used to know?"

"Wish I may die if she ain't the very spit of her," replied the man.

"Well, then," said Jane—and a thrill of joyful pride ran through her, "perhaps you know how to milk cows?"

"Perhaps I does," was the burglar's cautious rejoinder.

"Then," said Jane, "if you will *only* milk ours—you don't know how we shall always love you."

The burglar replied that loving was all very well.

"If those cats only had a good long wet thirsty drink of milk," Jane went on, with eager persuasion, "they'd lie down and go to sleep as likely as not, and then the police won't come back. But if they go on mewing like this he will, and then I don't know what'll become of us, or you either."

This argument seemed to decide the criminal. Jane fetched the washbowl from the sink, and he spat on his hands and prepared to milk the cow. At this instant boots were heard on the stairs.

"It's all up," said the man, desperately, "this 'ere's a plant. '*Ere's* the police." He made as if to open the window and leap from it.

"It's all right, I tell you," whispered Jane in anguish. "I'll say you're a friend of mine, or the good clergyman called in, or my uncle, or *anything*—only do, do, do milk the cow. Oh, *don't go*—oh—oh, thank goodness, it's only the boys!"

It was; and their entrance had awakened Anthea, who, with her brothers, now crowded through the doorway. The man looked about him like a rat looks round a trap.

"This is a friend of mine," said Jane. "He's just called in, and he's going to milk the cow for us. *Isn't* it good and kind of him?"

She winked at the others, and though they did not understand they played up loyally.

"How do?" said Cyril. "Very glad to meet you. Don't let us interrupt the milking."

"I shall 'ave a 'ead and a 'arf in the morning, and no bloomin' error," remarked the burglar; but he began to milk the cow.

Robert was winked at to stay and see that he did not leave off milking or try to escape, and the others went to get things to put the milk in; for it was now spurting and foaming in the washbowl, and the cats had ceased from mewing and were crowding round the cow, with expressions of hope and anticipation in their whiskered faces.

"We can't get rid of any more cats," said Cyril, as he and his sisters piled a tray high with saucers and soup plates, and platters and pie dishes, "the police nearly got us as it was. Not the same one—a much stronger sort. He thought it really was a foundling orphan we'd got. If it hadn't been for me throwing the two bags of cat slap in his eye and hauling Robert over a railing, and lying like mice under a laurel bush— Well, it's jolly lucky I'm a good shot, that's all. He pranced off when he'd got the cat bags off his face—thought we'd bolted. And here we are."

The gentle samishness of the milk swishing into the handbowl seemed to have soothed the burglar very much. He went on milking in a sort of happy dream, while the children got a cup and ladled the warm milk out into the pie dishes and plates, and platters and saucers, and set them down to the music of Persian purrs and lappings.

"It makes me think of old times," said the burglar, smearing his ragged coat cuffs across his eyes, "about the apples in the orchard at home, and the rats at threshing time, and the rabbits and the ferrets, and how pretty it was seeing the pigs killed."

Finding him in this softened mood, Jane said:

"I wish you'd tell us how you came to choose our house for your burglaring tonight. I am awfully glad you did. You *have* been so kind. I don't know what we should have done without you," she added hastily. "We all love you ever so. Do tell us."

The others added their affectionate entreaties, and at last the burglar said:

"Well, it's my first job, and I didn't expect to be made so welcome, and that's the truth, young gents and ladies. And I don't know but what it won't be my last. For this 'ere cow, she reminds me of my father, and I know 'ow 'e'd 'ave 'ided me if I'd laid 'ands on a 'a'penny as wasn't my own."

"I'm sure he would," Jane agreed kindly. "But what made you come here?"

"Well, miss," said the burglar, "you know best 'ow you come by them cats, and why you don't like the police, so I'll give myself away free, and trust to your noble 'earts. (You'd best bale out a bit, the pan's getting fullish.) I was a-selling oranges off of my barrow—for I ain't a burglar by trade, though you 'ave used the name so free—an' there was a lady bought three 'a'porth off me. An' while she was a pickin' of them out—very careful indeed, and I'm always glad when them sort gets a few overripe ones—there was two other ladies talkin' over the fence. An' one on 'em said to the other on 'em, just like this:

" 'I've told both gells to come, and they can doss in with M'ria and Jane, 'cause their boss and his missis is miles away and the kids too. So they can just lock up the 'ouse and leave the gas a-burning, so's no one won't know, and get back bright an' early by 'leven o'clock. And we'll make a night of it, Mrs. Prosser, so we will. I'm just a-going to run out to pop the letter in the post.' And then the lady what had chosen the three ha'porth so careful, she said: 'Lor', Mrs. Wigson, I wonder at you, and your hands all over suds. This good gentleman'll slip it into the post for yer, I'll be bound, seeing I'm a customer of his.' So they give me the letter, and of course I read the direction what was written on it afore I shove it into the post. And then when I'd sold my barrowful, I was a-goin' 'ome with the chink in my pocket, and I'm blowed if some bloomin' thievin' beggar didn't nick the lot

whilst I was just a-wettin' of my whistle, for callin' of oranges
is dry work. Nicked the bloomin' lot 'e did—and me with
not a farden to take 'ome to my brother and his missus."

"How awful," said Anthea, with much sympathy.

"Horful indeed, miss, I believe yer," the burglar rejoined
with deep feeling. "You don't know her temper when she's
roused. An' I'm sure I 'ope you never may, neither. And I'd
'ad all my oranges off of 'em. So it came back to me what
was wrote on the ongverlope, and I says to myself, 'Why not,
seein' as I've been done myself, and if they keeps two slaveys
there must be some pickings?' An' so 'ere I am. But them
cats, they've brought me back to the ways of honestness.
Never no more."

"Look here," said Cyril, "these cats are very valuable—
very indeed. And we will give them all to you, if you will
take them away."

"I see they're a breedy lot," replied the burglar. "But I
don't want no bother with the coppers. Did you come by
them honest now? Straight?"

"They are all our very own," said Anthea. "We wanted
them, but the confidement—"

"Consignment," whispered Cyril.

"—was larger than we wanted, and they're an awful
bother. If you got your barrow, and some sacks or baskets,
your brother's missus would be awfully pleased. My father
says Persian cats are worth pounds and pounds each."

"Well," said the burglar—and he was certainly moved by
her remarks, "I see you're in a hole—and I don't mind
lending a helping 'and. I don't ask 'ow you come by them.
But I've got a pal—'e's a mark on cats. I'll fetch him along,

and if he thinks they'd fetch anything above their skins I don't mind doin' you a kindness."

"You won't go away and never come back," said Jane, "because I don't think I *could* bear that."

The burglar, quite touched by her emotion, swore sentimentally that, alive or dead, he would come back.

Then he went, and Cyril and Robert sent the girls to bed and sat up to wait for his return. It soon seemed absurd to await him in a state of wakefulness, but his stealthy tap on the window awoke them readily enough. For he did return, with the pal and the barrow and the sacks. The pal approved of the cats, now dormant in Persian repletion, and they were bundled into the sacks, and taken away on the barrow— mewing, indeed, but with mews too sleepy to attract public attention.

"I'm a fence—that's what I am," said the burglar gloomily. "I never thought I'd come down to this, and all acause er my kind 'eart."

Cyril knew that a fence is a receiver of stolen goods, and he replied briskly:

"I give you my sacred the cats aren't stolen. What do you make the time?"

"I ain't got the time on me," said the pal, "but it was just about chucking-out time as I came by the Bull and Gate. I shouldn't wonder if it was nigh upon one now."

When the cats had been removed, and the boys and the burglar had parted with warm expressions of friendship, there remained only the cow.

"She must stay all night," said Robert. "Cook'll have a fit when she sees her."

"All night?" said Cyril. "Why—it's tomorrow morning if it's one. We can have another wish!"

So the carpet was urged, in a hastily written note, to remove the cow to wherever she belonged and to return to its proper place on the nursery floor. But the cow could not be got to move on to the carpet. So Robert got the clothesline out of the back kitchen and tied one end very firmly to the cow's horns, and the other end to a bunched-up corner of the carpet, and said, "Fire away."

And the carpet and cow vanished together, and the boys went to bed, tired out and only too thankful that the evening at last was over.

Next morning the carpet lay calmly in its place, but one corner was very badly torn. It was the corner that the cow had been tied on to.

# Chapter 9

# The Burglar's Bride

*T*he morning after the adventure of the Persian cats, the muskrats, the common cow, and the uncommon burglar, all the children slept till it was ten o'clock, and then it was only Cyril who woke; but he attended to the others, so that by half-past ten everyone was ready to help to get breakfast. It was shivery cold, and there was but little in the house that was really worth eating.

Robert had arranged a thoughtful little surprise for the absent servants. He had made a neat and delightful booby trap over the kitchen door, and as soon as they heard the front door click open and knew the servants had come back, all four children hid in the cupboard under the stairs and listened with delight to the entrance—the tumble, the splash, the scuffle, and the remarks of the servants. They heard the cook say it was a judgment on them for leaving the place to itself; she seemed to think that a booby trap was a kind of plant that was quite likely to grow, all by itself, in a dwelling that was left shut up. But the housemaid, more acute, judged that someone must have been in the house—a view confirmed by the sight of the breakfast things on the nursery table.

The cupboard under the stairs was very tight and paraffiny, however, and a silent struggle for a place on top ended in the door bursting open and discharging Jane, who rolled like a football to the feet of the servants.

"Now," said Cyril firmly, when the cook's hysterics had become quieter and the housemaid had time to say what she thought of them, "don't you begin jawing us. We aren't going to stand it. We know too much. You'll please make an extra special treacle roley for dinner, and we'll have a tinned tongue."

"I daresay," said the housemaid, indignant, still in her outdoor things and with her hat very much on one side. "Don't you come a-threatening me, Master Cyril, because I won't stand it, so I tell you. You tell your ma about us being out? Much I care! She'll be sorry for me when she hears about my dear great-aunt by marriage as brought me up from a child and was a mother to me. She sent for me, she did, she wasn't expected to last the night, from the spasms going to her legs—and Cook was that kind and careful she couldn't let me go alone, so—"

"Don't," said Anthea, in real distress. "You know where liars go to, Eliza—at least if you don't—"

"Liars indeed!" said Eliza. "I won't demean myself talking to you."

"How's Mrs. Wigson?" said Robert. "And *did* you keep it up last night?"

The mouth of the housemaid fell open.

"Did you doss with Maria or Emily?" asked Cyril.

"How did Mrs. Prosser enjoy herself?" asked Jane.

"Forbear," said Cyril, "they've had enough. Whether we tell or not depends on your later life," he went on, addressing the servants. "If you are decent to us we'll be decent to you. You'd better make that treacle roley—and if I were you, Eliza, I'd do a little housework and cleaning, just for a change."

The servants gave in once and for all.

"There's nothing like firmness," Cyril went on, when the breakfast things were cleared away and the children were alone in the nursery. "People are always talking of difficulties with servants. It's quite simple, when you know the way. We can do what we like now and they won't peach. I think we've broken *their* proud spirit. Let's go somewhere by carpet."

"I wouldn't if I were you," said the Phoenix, yawning, as it swooped down from its roost on the curtain pole. "I've given you one or two hints, but now concealment is at an end, and I see I must speak out."

It perched on the back of a chair and swayed to and fro, like a parrot on a swing.

"What's the matter now?" said Anthea. She was not quite so gentle as usual, because she was still weary from the excitement of last night's cats. "I'm tired of things happening. I shan't go anywhere on the carpet. I'm going to darn my stockings."

"Darn!" said the Phoenix. "Darn! From those young lips these strange expressions—"

"Mend, then," said Anthea, "with a needle and wool."

The Phoenix opened and shut its wings thoughtfully.

"Your stockings," it said, "are much less important than they now appear to you. But the carpet—look at the bare worn patches, look at the great rent at yonder corner. The carpet has been your faithful friend—your willing servant. How have you requited its devoted service?"

"Dear Phoenix," Anthea urged, "don't talk in that horrid lecturing tone. You make me feel as if I'd done something wrong. And really it *is* a wishing carpet, and we haven't done anything else to it—only wishes."

"Only wishes," repeated the Phoenix, ruffling its neck feathers angrily, "and what sort of wishes? Wishing people to be in a good temper, for instance. What carpet did you ever hear of that had such a wish asked of it? But this noble fabric, on which you trample so recklessly"—everyone removed his boots from the carpet and stood on the linoleum— "this carpet never flinched. It did what you asked, but the wear and tear must have been awful. And then last night—I don't blame you about the cats and rats, for those were its own choice; but what carpet could stand a heavy cow hanging on to it at one corner?"

"I should think the cats and rats were worse," said Robert. "Look at all their claws—"

"Yes," said the bird, "eleven thousand nine hundred and forty of them—I daresay you noticed? I should be surprised if these had not left their mark."

"Good gracious," said Jane, sitting down suddenly on the floor and patting the edge of the carpet softly, "do you mean it's *wearing out?*"

"It's life with you has not been a luxurious one," said the Phoenix. "French mud twice. Sand of sunny shores twice. Soaking in southern seas once. India once. Goodness knows where in Persia once. Muskratland once. And once, wherever the cow came from. Hold your carpet up to the light, and with cautious tenderness, if *you* please."

With cautious tenderness the boys held the carpet up to the light; the girls looked, and a shiver of regret ran through them as they saw how those eleven thousand nine hundred and forty claws had run through the carpet. It was full of little holes: There were some large ones, and more than one thin place. At one corner a strip of it was torn, and hung forlornly.

"We must mend it," said Anthea. "Never mind about my stockings. I can sew them up in lumps with sewing cotton if there's no time to do them properly. I know it's awful and no girl would who respected herself, and all that; but the poor dear carpet's more important than my silly stockings. Let's go out now this very minute."

So out they all went and bought wool to mend the carpet; but there is no shop in Camden Town where you can buy wishing wool, no, nor in Kentish Town either. However, ordinary Scotch heather mixture fingering seemed good enough, and this they bought, and all that day Jane and Anthea darned and darned and darned. The boys went out for a walk in the afternoon, and the gentle Phoenix paced up and down the table—for exercise, as it said—and talked to the industrious girls about their carpet.

"It is not an ordinary, ignorant, innocent carpet from Kidderminster," it said, "it is a carpet with a past—a Persian past. Do you know that in happier years, when that carpet was the property of caliphs, viziers, kings, and sultans, it never lay on a floor?"

"I thought the floor was the proper home of a carpet," Jane interrupted.

"Not of a *magic* carpet," said the Phoenix. "Why, if it had been allowed to lie about on floors there wouldn't be much of it left now. No, indeed! It has lived in chests of cedar-wood, inlaid with pearl and ivory, wrapped in priceless tissues of cloth of gold, embroidered with gems of fabulous value. It has reposed in the sandalwood caskets of princesses, and in the rose-attar–scented treasurehouses of kings. Never, never, had anyone degraded it by walking on it—except in the way of business, when wishes were required, and then they always took their shoes off. And *you*—"

"Oh, *don't!*" said Jane, very near tears. "You know you'd never have been hatched at all if it hadn't been for Mother wanting a carpet for us to walk on."

"You needn't have walked so much or so hard!" said the bird, "but come, dry that crystal tear, and I will relate to you the story of the Princess Zulieka, the Prince of Asia, and the magic carpet."

"Relate away," said Anthea. "I mean, please do."

"The Princess Zulieka, fairest of royal ladies," began the bird, "had in her cradle been the subject of several enchantments. Her grandmother had been in her day—"

But what in her day Zulieka's grandmother had been was destined never to be revealed, for Cyril and Robert suddenly burst into the room, and on each brow were the traces of deep emotion. On Cyril's pale brow stood beads of agitation and perspiration, and on the scarlet brow of Robert was a large black smear.

"What ails ye both?" asked the Phoenix, and it added tartly that storytelling was quite impossible if people would come interrupting like that.

"Oh, do shut up, for any sake!" said Cyril, sinking into a chair.

Robert smoothed the ruffled golden feathers, adding kindly:

"Squirrel doesn't mean to be a beast. It's only that the *most awful* thing has happened, and stories don't seem to matter so much. Don't be cross. You won't be when you've heard what's happened."

"Well, what *has* happened?" said the bird, still rather crossly; and Anthea and Jane paused with long needles poised in air, and long needlefuls of Scotch heather mixture fingering wool drooping from them.

"The most awful thing you can possibly think of," said Cyril. "That nice chap—our own burglar—the police have got him, on suspicion of stolen cats. That's what his brother's missus told me."

"Oh, begin at the beginning!" cried Anthea impatiently.

"Well, then, we went out, and down by where the undertaker's is with the china flowers in the window—you know. There was a crowd, and of course we went to have a squint. And it was two bobbies and our burglar between them, and he was being dragged along; and he said, 'I tell you them cats was *give* me. I got 'em in exchange for me milking a cow in a basement parlor up Camden Town way.'

"And the people laughed. Beasts! And then one of the policemen said perhaps he could give the name and address of the cow, and he said, no, he couldn't; but he could take them there if they'd only leave go of his coat collar and give him a chance to get his breath. And the policeman said he could tell all that to the magistrate in the morning. He didn't see us, and so we came away."

"Oh, Cyril, how *could* you?" said Anthea.

"Don't be a pudding-head," Cyril advised. "A fat lot of good it would have done if we'd let him see us. No one would have believed a word we said. They'd have thought we were kidding. We did better than let him see us. We asked a boy where he lived and he told us, and we went there, and it's a little greengrocer's shop, and we bought some Brazil nuts. Here they are." The girls waved away the Brazil nuts with loathing and contempt.

"Well, we had to buy *something*, and while we were making up our minds what to buy we heard his brother's missus talking. She said when he came home with all them miaoulers she thought there was more in it than met the eye. But he *would* go out this morning with the two likeliest of them, one under each arm. She said he sent her out to buy blue ribbon to put round their beastly necks, and she said if he got three months' hard it was her dying word that he'd got the blue ribbon to thank for it; that, and his own silly thieving ways, taking cats that anybody would know he couldn't have come by in the way of business, instead of things that wouldn't have been missed, which Lord knows there are plenty such, and—"

"Oh, STOP!" cried Jane. And indeed it was time, for Cyril seemed like a clock that had been wound up and could not help going on. "Where is he now?"

"At the police station," said Robert, for Cyril was out of breath. "The boy told us they'd put him in the cells and would bring him up before the Beak in the morning. I thought it was a jolly lark last night—getting him to take the cats—but now . . . "

"The end of a lark," said the Phoenix, "is the Beak."

"Let's go to him," cried both the girls, jumping up. "Let's go and tell the truth. They *must* believe us."

"They *can't*," said Cyril. "Just think! If anyone came to

you with such a tale, you couldn't believe it, however much
you tried. We should only mix things up worse for him."

"There must be something we could do," said Jane, sniffing very much. "My own dear pet burglar! I can't bear it.
And he was so nice, the way he talked about his father, and
how he was going to be so extra honest. Dear Phoenix, you
_must_ be able to help us. You're so good and kind and pretty
and clever. Do, do, tell us what to do!"

The Phoenix rubbed its beak throughtfully with its claw.

"You might rescue him," it said, "and conceal him here,
till the law supporters had forgotten about him."

"That would be ages and ages," said Cyril, "and we couldn't
conceal him here. Father might come home at any moment,
and if he found the burglar here _he_ wouldn't believe the true
truth any more than the police would. That's the worst of
the truth. Nobody ever believes it. Couldn't we take him
somewhere else?"

Jane clapped her hands.

"The sunny southern shore," she cried, "where the cook is
being queen. He and she would be company for each other!"

And really the idea did not seem bad, if only he would
consent to go.

So, all talking at once, the children arranged to wait till
evening, and then to seek the dear burglar in his lonely cell.

Meanwhile Jane and Anthea darned away as hard as they
could, to make the carpet as strong as possible. For all felt
how terrible it would be if the precious burglar, while being
carried to the sunny southern shore, were to tumble through
a hole in the carpet and be lost forever in the sunny southern
sea.

The servants were tired after Mrs. Wigson's party, so everyone went to bed early, and when the Phoenix reported that both servants were snoring in a heartfelt and candid manner, the children got up—they had never undressed; just putting their nightgowns on over their things had been enough to deceive Eliza when she came to turn out the gas. So they were ready for anything, and they stood on the carpet and said:

"I wish we were in our burglar's lonely cell," and instantly they were.

I think everyone had expected the cell to be the "deepest dungeon below the castle moat." I am sure no one had doubted that the burglar, chained by heavy fetters to a ring in the damp stone wall, would be tossing uneasily on a bed of straw, with a pitcher of water and a moldering crust, untasted, beside him. Robert, remembering the underground passage and the treasure, had brought a candle and matches, but these were not needed.

The cell was a little whitewashed room about twelve feet long and six feet wide. On one side of it was a sort of shelf sloping a little toward the wall. On this were two rugs, striped blue and yellow, and a waterproof pillow. Rolled in the rugs, and with his head on the pillow, lay the burglar, fast asleep. (He had had his tea, though this the children did not know—it had come from the coffeeshop round the corner, in very thick crockery.) The scene was plainly revealed by the light of a gas lamp in the passage outside, which shone into the cell through a pane of thick glass over the door.

"I shall gag him," said Cyril, "and Robert will hold him down. Anthea and Jane and the Phoenix can whisper soft nothings to him while he gradually awakes."

This plan did not have the success it deserved, because the burglar, curiously enough, was much stronger, even in his sleep, than Robert and Cyril, and at the first touch of their hands he leapt up and shouted out something very loud indeed.

Instantly steps were heard outside. Anthea threw her arms round the burglar and whispered:

"It's us—the ones that gave you the cats. We've come to save you, only don't let on we're here. Can't we hide somewhere?"

Heavy boots sounded on the flagged passage outside and a firm voice shouted.

"Here—you—stop that row, will you?"

"All right, governor," replied the burglar, still with Anthea's arms round him. "I was only a-talkin' in my sleep. No offense."

It was an awful moment. Would the boots and the voice come in? Yes! No! The voice said:

"Well, stow it, will you?"

And the boots went heavily away, along the passage and up some sounding stone stairs.

"Now then," whispered Anthea.

"How the blue Moses did you get in?" asked the burglar in a hoarse whisper of amazement.

"On the carpet," said Jane, truly.

"Stow that," said the burglar. "One on you I could 'a swallowed, but four—and a yellow fowl."

"Look here," said Cyril sternly, "you wouldn't have believed anyone if they'd told you beforehand about your finding a cow and all those cats in our nursery."

"That I wouldn't," said the burglar with whispered fervor, "so help me Bob, I wouldn't."

"Well then," Cyril went on, ignoring this appeal to his brother, "just try to believe what we tell you and act accordingly. It can't do you any *harm*, you know," he went on in hoarse whispered earnestness. "You can't be very much worse off than you are now, you know. But if you'll just trust to us we'll get you out of this right enough. No one saw us come in. The question is, Where would you like to go?"

"I'd like to go to Boolong," was the instant reply of the burglar. "I've always wanted to go on that there trip, but I've never 'ad the ready at the right time of year."

"Boolong is a town like London," said Cyril, well-meaning but inaccurate. "How could you get a living there?"

"It's 'ard to get a 'onest living anywheres nowadays," he said, and his voice was sad.

"Yes, isn't it?" said Jane sympathetically. "But how about a sunny southern shore, where there's nothing to do at all unless you want to?"

"That's my billet, miss," replied the burglar. "I never did care about work—not like some people, always fussing about."

"Did you never like any sort of work?" asked Anthea severely.

"Lor', lumme, yes," he answered. "Gardening was my 'obby, so it was. But Father died afore 'e could bind me to a nurseryman, an'—"

"We'll take you to the sunny southern shore," said Jane. "You've no idea what the flowers are like."

"Our old cook's there," said Anthea. "She's queen—"

"Oh, chuck it," the burglar whispered, clutching at his head with both hands. "I knowed the first minute I see them cats and that cow as it was a judgment on me. I don't know now whether I'm a-standing on my hat or my boots, so help me I don't. If you *can* get me out, get me, and if you can't, get along with you for goodness' sake, and give me a chanst to think about what'll be most likely to go down with the Beak in the morning."

"Come on to the carpet, then," said Anthea, gently shoving. The others quietly pulled, and the moment the feet of the burglar were planted on the carpet Anthea wished: "I wish we were all on the sunny southern shore where Cook is." And instantly they were. There were the rainbow sands, the tropic glories of leaf and flower, and there, of course, was the cook, crowned with white flowers, and with all the wrinkles of crossness and tiredness and hard work wiped out of her face.

"Why, Cook, you're quite pretty!" Anthea said, as soon as she had got her breath after the tumble-rush-whirl of the carpet. The burglar stood rubbing his eyes in the brilliant tropic sunlight and gazing wildly round him on the vivid hues of the tropic land.

"Penny plain and tuppence colored!" he exclaimed pensively. "And well worth any tuppence, however hard-earned."

The cook was seated on a grassy mound with her court of copper-colored savages around her. The burglar pointed a grimy finger at these.

"Are they tame?" he asked anxiously. "Do they bite or scratch, or do anything to yer with poisoned arrows or oyster shells or that?"

"Don't you be so timid," said the cook. "Look'e 'ere, this 'ere's only a dream what you've come into, an' as it's only a dream there's no nonsense about what a young lady like me ought to say or not, so I'll say you're the best-looking fellow I've seen this many a day. And the dream goes on and on, seemingly, as long as you behaves. The things what you has to eat and drink tastes just as good as real ones, and—"

"Look 'ere," said the burglar, "I've come 'ere straight outer the pleece station. These 'ere kids'll tell you it ain't no blame er mine."

"Well, you *were* a burglar, you know," said the truthful Anthea gently.

"Only because I was druv to it by dishonest blokes, as well you knows, miss," rejoined the criminal. "Blowed if this ain't the 'ottest January as I've known for years."

"Wouldn't you like a bath?" asked the queen. "And some white clothes like me?"

"I should only look a juggins in 'em, miss, thanking you all the same" was the reply. "But a bath I wouldn't resist, and my shirt was only clean on week before last."

Cyril and Robert led him to a rocky pool, where he bathed luxuriously. Then, in shirt and trousers, he sat on the sand and spoke.

"That cook, or queen, or whatever you call her—her with the white bokay on her 'ed—she's my sort. Wonder if she'd keep company!"

"I should ask her."

"I was always a quick hitter," the man went on. "It's a word and a blow with me. I will."

In shirt and trousers, and crowned with a scented flowery wreath which Cyril hastily wove as they returned to the court of the queen, the burglar stood before the cook and spoke.

"Look 'ere, miss," he said. "You an' me bein' all forlornlike, both on us, in this 'ere dream, or whatever you calls it, I'd like to tell you straight as I likes yer looks."

The cook smiled and looked down bashfully.

"I'm a single man—what you might call a batcheldore. I'm mild in my 'abits, which these kids'll tell you the same, and I'd like to'ave the pleasure of walkin' out with you next Sunday."

"Lor'," said the queen-cook, " 'ow sudden you are, mister."

"Walking out means you're going to be married," said Anthea. "Why not get married and have done with it? I would—"

"I don't mind if I do," said the burglar.

But the cook said, "No, miss. Not me, not even in a dream. I don't say anthink ag'in the young chap's looks, but I always swore I'd be married in church, if at all—and, anyway, I don't believe these here savages would know how to keep a registering office, even if I was to show them. No, mister, thanking you kindly, if you can't bring a clergyman into the dream I'd live and die like what I am."

"Will you marry her if we get a clergyman?" asked the matchmaking Anthea.

"I'm agreeable, miss, I'm sure," said he, pulling his wreath straight. " 'Ow this 'ere bokay do tiddle a chap's ears to be sure!"

So, very hurriedly, the carpet was spread out and instructed to fetch a clergyman. The instructions were written on the inside of Cyril's cap with a piece of billiard chalk Robert had got from the marker at the hotel at Lyndhurst. The carpet disappeared, and more quickly than you would have thought possible it came back, bearing on its bosom the Reverend Septimus Blenkinsop.

The Reverend Septimus was rather a nice young man, but very much mazed and muddled, because when he saw a strange carpet laid out at his feet, in his own study, he naturally walked on to it to examine it more closely. And he happened to stand on one of the thin places that Jane and Anthea had darned, so that he was half on wishing carpet and half on plain Scotch heather mixture fingering, which has no magic properties at all.

The effect of this was that he was only half there—so that the children could just see through him, as though he had been a ghost. And as for him, he saw the sunny southern shore, the cook and the burglar and the children, quite plainly; but through them all he saw, quite plainly also, his study at home, with the books and the pictures and the marble clock that had been presented to him when he left his last situation.

He seemed to himself to be in a sort of insane fit, so that it did not matter what he did—and he married the burglar to the cook. The cook said that she would rather have had a solider kind of clergyman, one that you couldn't see through so plain, but perhaps this was real enough for a dream.

And of course the clergyman, though misty, was really real, and able to marry people, and he did. When the ceremony was over the clergyman wandered about the island collecting botanical specimens, for he was a great botanist, and the ruling passion was strong even in an insane fit.

There was a splendid wedding feast. Can you fancy Jane and Anthea, and Robert and Cyril, dancing merrily in a ring, hand in hand with copper-colored savages, round the happy couple, the queen-cook and the burglar consort? There were more flowers gathered and thrown than you have ever even dreamed of, and before the children took carpet for home the now married-and-settled burglar made a speech.

"Ladies and gentlemen," he said, "and savages of both kinds, only I know you can't understand what I'm saying of, but we'll let that pass. If this is a dream, I'm on. If it ain't, I'm onner than ever. If it's betwixt and between—well, I'm honest, and I can't say more. I don't want no more 'igh London society—I've got someone to put my arm around of; and I've got the whole lot of this 'ere island for my allotment, and if I don't grow some broccoli as'll open the judge's eye at the cottage flower shows, well, strike me pink! All I ask is, as these young gents and ladies'll bring some parsley seed into the dream, and a penn'orth o' radish seed, and threepenn'orth of onion, and I wouldn't mind goin' to fourpence or fippence for mixed kale, only I ain't got a brown, so I don't deceive you. And there's one thing more, you might take away the parson. I don't like things what I can see 'alf through, so here's how!" He drained a coconut shell of palm wine.

It was now past midnight—though it was teatime on the island.

With all good wishes the children took their leave. They also collected the clergyman and took him back to his study and his presentation clock.

The Phoenix kindly carried the seeds next day to the burglar and his bride, and returned with the most satisfactory news of the happy pair.

"He's made a wooden spade and started on his allotment," it said, "and she is weaving him a shirt and trousers of the most radiant whiteness."

The police never knew how the burglar got away. In

Kentish Town Police Station his escape is still spoken of with bated breath as the Persian mystery.

As for the Reverend Septimus Blenkinsop, he felt that he had had a very insane fit indeed, and he was sure it was due to overstudy. So he planned a little dissipation, and took his two maiden aunts to Paris, where they enjoyed a dazzling round of museums and picture galleries, and came back feeling that they had indeed seen life. He never told his aunts or anyone else about the marriage on the island—because no one likes it to be generally known if he has had insane fits, however interesting and unusual.

# Chapter 10

# The Hole in the Carpet

"Hooray! hooray! hooray!
Mother comes home today;
Mother comes home today,
Hooray! hooray! hooray!"

**J**ane sang this simple song directly after breakfast, and the Phoenix shed crystal tears of affectionate sympathy.

"How beautiful," it said, "is filial devotion!"

"She won't be home till past bedtime, though," said Robert. "We might have one more carpet day."

He was glad that mother was coming home—quite glad, very glad; but at the same time that gladness was rudely contradicted by a quite strong feeling of sorrow, because now they could not go out all day on the carpet.

"I do wish we could go and get something nice for Mother, only she'd want to know where we got it," said Anthea. "And she'd never, never believe the truth. People never do, somehow, if it's at all interesting."

"I'll tell you what," said Robert. "Suppose we wished the carpet to take us somewhere where we could find a purse with money in it—then we could buy her something."

"Suppose it took us somewhere foreign, and the purse was covered with strange Eastern devices, embroidered in rich silks, and full of money that wasn't money at all here, only foreign curiosities, then we couldn't spend it, and people would bother about where we got it, and we shouldn't know how on earth to get out of it at all." Cyril moved the table off the carpet as he spoke, and its leg caught in one of Anthea's darns and ripped away most of it, as well as a large slit in the carpet.

"Well, now you *have* done it," said Robert.

But Anthea was a really first-class sister. She did not say a word till she had got out the Scotch heather mixture finger-ing wool, and the darning needle and the thimble and the scissors, and by that time she had been able to get the better of her natural wish to be thoroughly disagreeable and was able to say quite kindly:

"Never mind, Squirrel, I'll soon mend it."

Cyril thumped her on the back. He understood exactly how she felt, and he was not an ungrateful brother.

"Respecting the purse containing coins," the Phoenix said, scratching its invisible ear thoughtfully with its shining claw, "it might be as well, perhaps, to state clearly the amount which you wish to find, as well as the country where you wish to find it, and the nature of the coins which you prefer. It would be indeed a cold moment when you should find a purse containing three oboloi."

"How much is an oboloi?"

"An obol is about twopence halfpenny," the Phoenix replied.

"Yes," said Jane, "and if you find a purse I suppose it is only because someone has lost it, and you ought to take it to the policeman."

"The situation," remarked the Phoenix, "does indeed bristle with difficulties."

"What about a buried treasure," said Cyril, "and everyone was dead that it belonged to?"

"Mother wouldn't believe *that*," said more than one voice.

"Suppose," said Robert, "suppose we asked to be taken where we could find a purse and give it back to the person it belonged to, and they would give us something for finding it?"

"We aren't allowed to take money from strangers. You know we aren't, Bobs," said Anthea, making a knot at the end of a needleful of Scotch heather mixture fingering wool (which is very wrong, and you must never do it when you are darning).

"No, *that* wouldn't do," said Cyril. "Let's chuck it and go to the North Pole, or somewhere really interesting."

"No," said the girls together, "there must be *some* way."

"Wait a sec," Anthea added. "I've got an idea coming. Don't speak."

There was a silence as she paused with the darning needle in the air. Suddenly she spoke:

"I see. Let's tell the carpet to take us somewhere where we can get the money for Mother's present, and—and—and get it some way that she'll believe in and not think wrong."

"Well, I must say you are learning the way to get the most out of the carpet," said Cyril. He spoke more heartily and kindly than usual, because he remembered how Anthea had refrained from snarking him about tearing the carpet.

"Yes," said the Phoenix, "you certainly are. And you have to remember that if you take a thing out it doesn't stay in."

No one paid any attention to this remark at the time, but afterward everyone thought of it.

"Do hurry up, Panther," said Robert; and that was why Anthea did hurry up, and why the big darn in the middle of the carpet was all open and webby like a fishing net, not tight and close like woven cloth, which is what a good, well-behaved darn should be.

Then everyone put on its outdoor things, the Phoenix fluttered onto the mantelpiece and arranged its golden feathers in the glass, and all was ready. Everyone got onto the carpet.

"Please go slowly, dear carpet," Anthea began. "We like to see where we're going." And then she added the difficult wish that had been decided on.

Next moment the carpet, stiff and raftlike, was sailing over the roofs of Kentish Town.

"I wish— No, I don't mean that. I mean it's a *pity* we aren't higher up," said Anthea, as the edge of the carpet grazed a chimneypot.

"That's right. Be careful," said the Phoenix, in warning tones. "If you wish when you're on a wishing carpet, you *do* wish, and there's an end of it."

So for a short time no one spoke, and the carpet sailed on in calm magnificence over St. Pancras and King's Cross stations and over the crowded streets of Clerkenwell.

"We're going out Greenwich way," said Cyril as they

crossed the streak of rough, tumbled water that was the Thames. "We might go and have a look at the palace."

On and on the carpet swept, still keeping much nearer to the chimneypots than the children found at all comfortable. And then, just over New Cross, a terrible thing happened.

Jane and Robert were in the middle of the carpet. Part of them was on the carpet, and part of them—the heaviest part—was on the great central darn.

"It's all very misty," said Jane. "It looks partly like out of doors and partly like in the nursery at home. I feel as if I was going to have measles; everything looked awfully rum then, I remember."

"I feel just exactly the same," Robert said.

"It's the hole," said the Phoenix. "It's not measles, whatever that possession may be."

And at that both Robert and Jane suddenly, and at once, made a bound to try and get onto the safer part of the carpet, and the darn gave way and their boots went up, and the heavy heads and bodies of them went down through the hole, and they landed in a position something between sitting and sprawling on the flat leads on the tip of a high, gray, gloomy, respectable house whose address was 705, Amersham Road, New Cross.

The carpet seemed to awaken to new energy as soon as it had got rid of their weight, and it rose high in the air. The others lay down flat and peered over the edge of the rising carpet.

"Are you hurt?" cried Cyril, and Robert shouted "No," and the next moment the carpet had sped away, and Jane and Robert were hidden from the sight of the others by a stack of smoky chimneys.

"Oh, how awful!" said Anthea.

"It might have been worse," said the Phoenix. "What would have been the sentiments of the survivors if that darn had given way when we were crossing the river?"

"Yes, there's that," said Cyril, recovering himself. "They'll be all right. They'll howl till someone gets them down, or drop tiles into the front garden to attract the attention of passersby. Bobs has got my one and fivepence—lucky you forgot to mend that hole in my pocket, Panther, or he wouldn't have had it. They can tram it home."

But Anthea would not be comforted.

"It's all my fault," she said. "I *knew* the proper way to darn, and I didn't do it. It's all my fault. Let's go home and patch the carpet with your Etons—something really strong—and send it to fetch them."

"All right," said Cyril, "but your Sunday jacket is stronger than my Etons. We must just chuck mother's present, that's all. I wish—"

"Stop!" cried the Phoenix. "The carpet is dropping to earth."

And indeed it was.

It sank swiftly, yet steadily, and landed on the pavement of the Deptford Road. It tipped a little as it landed, so that Cyril and Anthea naturally walked off it, and in an instant it had rolled itself up and hidden behind a gatepost. It did this so quickly that not a single person in the Deptford Road noticed it. The Phoenix rustled its way into the breast of Cyril's coat, and almost at the same moment a well-known voice remarked:

"Well, I never! What on earth are you doing here?"

They were face to face with their pet uncle—their Uncle Reginald.

"We *did* think of going to Greenwich Palace and talking about Nelson," said Cyril, telling as much of the truth as he thought his uncle could believe.

"And where are the others?" asked Uncle Reginald.

"I don't exactly know," Cyril replied, this time quite truthfully.

"Well," said Uncle Reginald, "I must fly. I've a case in the County Court. That's the worst of being a beastly solicitor. One can't take the chances of life when one gets them. If only I could come with you to the Painted Hall and give you lunch at the Ship afterward! But, alas, it may not be."

The uncle felt in his pocket.

"*I* mustn't enjoy myself," he said, "but that's no reason why you shouldn't. Here, divide this by four, and the product ought to give you *some* desired result. Take care of yourselves. Adieu."

And waving a cheery farewell with his neat umbrella, the good and high-hatted uncle passed away, leaving Cyril and Anthea to exchange eloquent glances over the shining golden sovereign that lay in Cyril's hand.

"Well!" said Anthea.

"Well!" said Cyril.

"Well!" said the Phoenix.

"Good old carpet!" said Cyril joyously.

"It *was* clever of it—so adequate and yet so simple," said the Phoenix with calm approval.

"Oh, come on home and let's mend the carpet. I am a beast. I'd forgotten the others just for a minute," said the conscience-stricken Anthea.

They unrolled the carpet quickly and slyly—they did not want to attract public attention—and the moment their feet were on the carpet Anthea wished to be at home, and instantly they were.

The kindness of their excellent uncle had made it unnecessary for them to go to such extremes as Cyril's Etons or Anthea's Sunday jacket for the patching of the carpet.

Anthea set to work at once to draw the edges of the broken darn together, and Cyril hastily went out and bought a large piece of the marble-patterned American oilcloth which careful housewives use to cover dressers and kitchen tables. It was the strongest thing he could think of.

Then they set to work to line the carpet throughout with the oilcloth. The nursery felt very odd and empty without the others, and Cyril did not feel so sure as he had done about their being able to "tram it" home. So he tried to help Anthea, which was very good of him, but not much use to her.

The Phoenix watched them for a time, but it was plainly growing more and more restless. It fluffed up its splendid feathers, and stood first on one gilded claw and then on the other, and at last it said:

"I can bear it no longer. This suspense! My Robert—who set my egg to hatch—in the bosom of whose Norfolk raiment I have nestled so often and so pleasantly! I think if you'll excuse me—"

"Yes—do," cried Anthea. "I wish we'd thought of asking you before."

Cyril opened the window. The Phoenix flapped its sun-bright wings and vanished.

"So *that's* all right," said Cyril, taking up his needle and instantly pricking his hand in a new place.

Of course I know that what you have really wanted to know about all this time is not what Anthea and Cyril did, but what happened to Jane and Robert after they fell through the carpet onto the leads of the house which was called number 705, Amersham Road.

But I had to tell you the other first. That is one of the most annoying things about stories, you cannot tell all the different parts of them at the same time.

Robert's first remark when he found himself seated on the damp, cold, sooty leads was:

"Here's a go!"

Jane's first act was tears.

"Dry up, Pussy; don't be a little duffer," said her brother kindly. "It'll be all right."

And then he looked about, just as Cyril had known he would, for something to throw down, so as to attract the attention of the wayfarers far below in the street. He could not find anything. Curiously enough, there were no stones on the leads, not even a loose tile. The roof was of slate, and every single slate knew its place and kept it. But, as so often happens, in looking for one thing he found another. There was a trapdoor leading down into the house.

And that trapdoor was not fastened.

"Stop sniveling and come here, Jane," he said encouragingly. "Lend a hand to heave this up. If we can get into the house, we might sneak down without meeting anyone, with luck. Come on."

They heaved up the door till it stood straight up, and, as

they bent to look into the hole below, the door fell back with a hollow clang on the leads behind, and with its noise was mingled a blood-curdling scream from underneath.

"Discovered!" hissed Robert. "Oh, my cats alive!"

They were indeed discovered.

They found themselves looking down into an attic, which was also a lumber room. It had boxes and broken chairs, old fenders and picture frames, and rag bags hanging from nails.

In the middle of the floor was a box, open, half full of clothes. Other clothes lay on the floor in neat piles. In the middle of the piles of clothes sat a lady, very flat indeed, with her feet sticking out straight in front of her. And it was she who had screamed and who, in fact, was still screaming.

"Don't!" cried Jane. "Please don't! We won't hurt you."

"Where are the rest of your gang?" asked the lady, stopping short in the middle of a scream.

"The others have gone on, on the wishing carpet," said Jane truthfully.

"The wishing carpet?" said the lady.

"Yes," said Jane, before Robert could say "You shut up!"

"You must have read about it. The Phoenix is with them."

Then the lady got up and, picking her way carefully between the piles of clothes, she got to the door and through it. She shut it behind her, and the two children could hear her calling, "Septimus! Septimus!" in a loud yet frightened way.

"Now," said Robert quickly. "I'll drop first."

He hung by his hands and dropped through the trapdoor.

"Now you. Hang by your hands. I'll catch you. Oh, there's no time for jaw. Drop, I say."

Jane dropped.

Robert tried to catch her, and even before they had finished the breathless roll among the piles of clothes, which was what his catching ended in, he whispered:

"We'll hide—behind those fenders and things; they'll think we've gone along the roofs. Then, when all is calm, we'll creep down the stairs and take our chance."

They hastily hid. A corner of an iron bedstead stuck into Robert's side, and Jane had only standing room for one foot—but they bore it—and when the lady came back, not with Septimus, but with another lady, they held their breaths and their hearts beat thickly.

"Gone!" said the first lady. "Poor little things—quite mad, my dear—and at large! We must lock this room and send for the police."

"Let me look out," said the second lady, who was, if possible, older and thinner and primmer than the first. So the two ladies dragged a box under the trapdoor and put another box on the top of it, and then they both climbed up very carefully and put their two trim, tidy heads out of the trapdoor to look for the "mad children."

"Now," whispered Robert, getting the bedstead leg out of his side.

They managed to creep out from their hiding place and out through the door before the two ladies had done looking out of the trapdoor on to the empty leads.

Robert and Jane tiptoed down the stairs—one flight, two flights. Then they looked over the banister. Horror! A servant was coming up with a loaded scuttle.

The children with one consent crept swiftly through the first open door.

The room was a study, calm and gentlemanly, with rows

of books, a writing table, and a pair of embroidered slippers warming themselves in the fender. The children hid behind the window curtains. As they passed the table they saw on it a missionary box with its bottom label torn off, open and empty.

"Oh, how awful!" whispered Jane. "We shall never get away alive."

"Hush!" said Robert, not a moment too soon, for there were steps on the stairs, and next instant the two ladies came into the room. They did not see the children, but they saw the empty missionary box.

"I knew it," said one. "Selina, it *was* a gang. I was certain of it from the first. The children were not mad. They were sent to distract our attention while their confederates robbed the house."

"I am afraid you are right," said Selina. "And *where are they now?*"

"Downstairs, no doubt, collecting the silver milk jug and sugar basin and the punch ladle that was Uncle Joe's, and Aunt Jerusha's teaspoons. I shall go down."

"Oh, don't be so rash and heroic," said Selina. "Amelia, we must call the police from the window. Lock the door. I *will*— I will—"

The words ended in a yell as Selina, rushing to the window, came face to face with the hidden children.

"Oh, don't!" said Jane. "How can you be so unkind? We *aren't* burglars, and we haven't any gang, and we didn't open your missionary box. We opened our own once, but we didn't have to use the money, so our consciences made us put it back and— *Don't!* Oh, I wish you wouldn't—"

Miss Selina had seized Jane and Miss Amelia captured

Robert. The children found themselves held fast by strong, slim hands, pink at the wrists, and white at the knuckles.

"We've got *you*, at any rate," said Miss Amelia. "Selina, your captive is smaller than mine. You open the window at once and call 'Murder!' as loud as you can."

Selina obeyed; but when she had opened the window, instead of calling "Murder" she called "Septimus!" because at that very moment she saw her nephew coming in at the gate.

In another minute he had let himself in with his latchkey and had mounted the stairs. As he came into the room Jane and Robert each uttered a shriek of joy so loud and so sudden that the ladies leapt with surprise, and nearly let them go.

"It's our own clergyman," cried Jane.

"Don't you remember us?" asked Robert. "You married our burglar for us—don't you remember?"

"I *knew* it was a gang," said Amelia. "Septimus, these abandoned children are members of a desperate burgling gang who are robbing the house. They have already forced the missionary box and purloined its contents."

The Reverend Septimus passed his hand wearily over his brow.

"I feel a little faint," he said, "running upstairs so quickly."

"We never touched the beastly box," said Robert.

"Then your confederates did," said Miss Selina.

"No, no," said the curate, hastily. "*I* opened the box myself. This morning I found I had not enough small change for the Mothers' Independent Unity Measles and Croup Insurance payments. I suppose this is *not* a dream, is it?"

"Dream? No, indeed. Search the house. I insist upon it."

The curate, still pale and trembling, searched the house, which of course, was blamelessly free of burglars.

When he came back he sank wearily into his chair.

"Aren't you going to let us go?" asked Robert, with furious indignation, for there is something in being held by a strong lady that sets the blood of a boy boiling in his veins with anger and despair. "We've never done anything to you. It's all the carpet. It dropped us on the leads. We couldn't help it. You know how it carried you over to the island, and you had to marry the burglar and the cook."

"Oh, my head!" said the curate.

"Never mind your head just now," said Robert. "Try to be honest and honorable, and do your duty in that state of life."

"This is a judgment on me for something, I suppose," said the Reverend Septimus wearily, "but I really cannot at the moment remember what."

"Send for the police," said Miss Selina.

"Send for the doctor," said the curate.

"Do you think they *are* mad, then?" said Miss Amelia.

"I think I am," said the curate.

Jane had been crying ever since her capture. Now she said:

"You aren't now, but perhaps you will be, if— And it would serve you jolly well right too."

"Aunt Selina," said the curate, "and Aunt Amelia, believe me, this is only an insane dream. You will realize it soon. It has happened to me before. But do not let us be unjust, even in a dream. Do not hold the children; they have done no harm. As I said before, it was I who opened the box."

The strong, bony hands unwillingly loosened their grasp. Robert shook himself and stood in sulky resentment. But Jane ran to the curate and embraced him so suddenly that he had not time to defend himself.

"You're a dear," she said. "It *is* like a dream just at first, but you get used to it. Now *do* let us go. There's a good, kind, honorable clergyman."

"I don't know," said the Reverend Septimus. "It's a difficult problem. It is such a very unusual dream. Perhaps it's only a sort of other life—quite real enough for you to be mad in. And if you're mad, there might be a dream asylum where you'd be kindly treated and in time restored, cured, to your sorrowing relatives. It is very hard to see your duty plainly, even in ordinary life, and these dream circumstances are so complicated—"

"If it's a dream," said Robert, "you will wake up directly, and then you'd be sorry if you'd sent us into a dream asylum, because you might never get into the same dream again and let us out, and so we might stay there forever, and then what about our sorrowing relatives who aren't in the dreams at all?"

But all the curate could say was "Oh, my head!"

And Jane and Robert felt quite ill with helplessness and hopelessness. A really conscientious curate is a very difficult thing to manage.

And then, just as the hopelessness and the helplessness were getting to be almost more than they could bear, the two children suddenly felt that extraordinary shrinking feeling that you always have when you are just going to vanish. And the next moment they had vanished, and the Reverend Septimus was left alone with his aunts.

"I knew it was a dream," he cried wildly. "I've had something like it before. Did you dream it too, Aunt Selina, and you, Aunt Amelia? I dreamed that you did, you know."

Aunt Selina looked at him and then at Aunt Amelia. Then she said boldly:

"What do you mean? *We* haven't been dreaming anything. You must have dropped off in your chair."

The curate heaved a sigh of relief.

"Oh, if it's only *I*," he said. "If we'd all dreamed it I could never have believed it, never!"

Afterward Aunt Selina said to the other aunt:

"Yes, I know it was an untruth, and I shall doubtless be punished for it in due course. But I could see the poor dear fellow's brain giving way before my very eyes. he couldn't have stood the strain of *three* dreams. It *was* odd, wasn't it? All three of us dreaming the same thing at the same moment. We must never tell dear Seppy. But I shall send an account of it to the Psychical Society, with stars instead of names, you know."

And she did. And you can read all about it in one of the society's fat blue books.


Of course, you understand what had happened?

The intelligent Phoenix had simply gone straight off to the Psammead and had wished Robert and Jane at home. And, of course, they were home at once. Cyril and Anthea had not half finished mending the carpet.

When the joyful emotions of reunion had calmed down a little they all went out and spent what was left of Uncle Reginald's sovereign in presents for Mother. They bought her a pink silk handkerchief, a pair of blue and white vases, a bottle of scent, a packet of Christmas candles, and a cake of soap shaped and colored like a tomato, and one that was so like an orange that almost anyone you had given it to would have tried to peel it—if they liked oranges, of course. Also they bought a cake with icing on, and the rest of the money they spent on flowers to put in the vases.

When they had arranged all the things on the table, with the candles stuck up on a plate ready to light the moment Mother's cab was heard, they washed themselves thoroughly and put on tidier clothes.

Then Robert said, "Good old Psammead," and the others said so too.

"But, really, it's just as much good old Phoenix," said Robert. "Suppose it hadn't thought of getting the wish!"

"Ah!" said the Phoenix. "It is perhaps fortunate for you that I am such a competent bird."

"There's Mother's cab," cried Anthea, and the Phoenix hid and they lighted the candles, and next moment Mother was home again.

She liked her presents very much, and found their story of Uncle Reginald and the sovereign easy and even pleasant to believe.

"Good old carpet," were Cyril's last sleepy words.

"What there is of it," said the Phoenix, from the cornice pole.

# Chapter 11

# The Beginning of the End

"**W**ell, I *must* say," Mother said, looking at the wishing carpet as it lay, all darned and mended and backed with shiny American cloth, on the floor of the nursery, "I *must* say I've never in my life bought such a bad bargain as that carpet."

A soft "Oh!" of contradiction sprang to the lips of Cyril, Robert, Jane, and Anthea. Mother looked at them quickly and said:

"Well, of course, I see you've mended it very nicely, and that was sweet of you, dears."

"The boys helped too," said the dears honorably.

"But, still—twenty-two and ninepence! It ought to have lasted for years. It's simply dreadful now. Well, never mind, darlings, you've done your best. I think we'll have coconut matting next time. A carpet doesn't have an easy life of it in this room, does it?"

"It's not our fault, Mother, is it, that our boots are the really reliable kind?" Robert asked the question more in sorrow than in anger.

"No, dear, we can't help our boots," said Mother cheerfully, "but we might change them when we come in, perhaps. It's just an idea of mine. I wouldn't dream of scolding on the very first morning after I've come home. Oh, my Lamb, how could you?"

This conversation was at breakfast, and the Lamb had been beautifully good until everyone was looking at the carpet, and then it was for him but the work of a moment to turn a glass dish of syrupy blackberry jam upside down on his young head. It was the work of a good many minutes and several persons to get the jam off him again, and this interesting work took people's minds off the carpet, and nothing more was said just then about its badness as a bargain and about what Mother hoped for from coconut matting.

When the Lamb was clean again he had to be taken care of while Mother rumpled her hair and inked her fingers and made her head ache over the difficult and twisted housekeeping accounts which Cook gave her on dirty bits of paper, and which were supposed to explain how it was that Cook had only fivepence-halfpenny and a lot of unpaid bills left out of all the money Mother had sent her for housekeeping. Mother was very clever, but even she could not quite understand the cook's accounts.

The Lamb was very glad to have his brothers and sisters to play with him. He had not forgotten them a bit, and he made them play all the old exhausting games: "Whirling Worlds," where you swing the baby round and round by his hands; and "Leg and Wing," where you swing him from side to side by one ankle and one wrist. There was also climbing Vesuvius. In this game the baby walks up you, and when he is standing on your shoulders, you shout as loud as you can, which is the rumbling of the burning mountain, and then tumble him gently on to the floor, and roll him there, which is the destruction of Pompeii.

"All the same, I wish we could decide what we'd better say next time Mother says anything about the carpet," said Cyril, breathlessly ceasing to be a burning mountain.

"Well, you talk and decide," said Anthea, "here, you lovey ducky Lamb. Come to Panther and play Noah's Ark."

The Lamb came with his pretty hair all tumbled and his face all dusty from the destruction of Pompeii, and instantly became a baby snake, hissing and wriggling and creeping in Anthea's arms, as she said:

> "I love my little baby snake,
> He hisses when he is awake,
> He creeps with such a wriggly creep,
> He wriggles even in his sleep . . ."

"Crocky," said the Lamb, and showed all his little teeth. So Anthea went on:

> "I love my little crocodile,
> I love his truthful, toothful smile;
> It is so wonderful and wide,
> I like to see it—*from outside*. . . ."

"Well, you see," Cyril was saying, "it's just the old bother, Mother can't believe the real truth about the carpet and—"

"You speak sooth, O Cyril," remarked the Phoenix, coming out from the cupboard where the black beetles lived, and the torn books, and the broken slates, and odd pieces of toys that had lost the rest of themselves. "Now hear the wisdom of the Phoenix, the son of the Phoenix."

"There is a society called that," said Cyril.

"Where is it? And what is a society?" asked the bird.

"It's a sort of joined-together lot of people—a sort of brotherhood—a kind of—well, something very like your temple, you know, and quite different."

"I take your meaning," said the Phoenix. "I would fain see these calling themselves Sons of the Phoenix."

"But what about your words of wisdom?"

"Wisdom is always welcome," said the Phoenix.

"Pretty Polly!" remarked the Lamb, reaching his hands toward the golden speaker.

The Phoenix modestly retreated behind Robert, and Anthea hastened to distract the attention of the Lamb by murmuring:

"I love my little baby rabbit;
But oh, he has a dreadful habit
Of paddling out among the rocks
And soaking both his bunny socks."

"I don't think you'd care about the Sons of the Phoenix, really," said Robert. "I have heard that they don't do anything fiery. They only drink a great deal. Much more than other people, because they drink lemonade and fizzy things, and the more you drink of those the more good you get."

"In your mind, perhaps," said Jane. "But it wouldn't be good in your body. You'd get too balloony."

The Phoenix yawned.

"Look here," said Anthea, "I really have an idea. This isn't like a common carpet. It's very magic indeed. Don't you think, if we put Tatcho on it and then gave it a rest, the magic part of it might grow, like hair is supposed to do?"

"It might," said Robert, "but I should think paraffin would do as well—at any rate as far as the smell goes, and that seems to be the great thing about Tatcho."

But with all its faults Anthea's idea was something to do, and they did it.

It was Cyril who fetched the Tatcho bottle from Father's washstand. But the bottle had not much in it.

"We mustn't take it all," Jane said, "in case Father's hair began to come off suddenly. If he hadn't anything to put on it, it might all drop off before Eliza had time to get round to the chemist's for another bottle. It would be dreadful to have a bald father, and it would all be our fault."

"And wigs are very expensive, I believe," said Anthea. "Look here, leave enough in the bottle to wet Father's head all over with in case any emergency emerges—and let's make up with paraffin. I expect it's the smell that does the good really—and the smell's exactly the same."

So a small teaspoonful of the Tatcho was put on the edges of the worst darn in the carpet and rubbed carefully into the roots of the hairs of it, and all the parts that there was not enough Tatcho for had paraffin rubbed into them with a piece of flannel. Then the flannel was burned. It made a gay flame, which delighted the Phoenix and the Lamb.

"How often," said Mother, opening the door, "how often am I to tell you that you are *not* to play with paraffin? What have you been doing?"

"We have burnt a paraffiny rag," Anthea answered.

It was no use telling Mother what they had done to the carpet. She did not know it was a magic carpet, and no one wants to be laughed at for trying to mend an ordinary carpet with lamp oil.

"Well, don't do it again," said Mother. "And now, away with melancholy! Father has sent a telegram. Look!" She held it out and the children, holding it by its yielding corners, read:

"Box for kiddies at Garrick. Stalls for us, Haymarket. Meet Charing Cross, 6:30."

"That means," said Mother, "that you're going to see *The Water Babies* all by your happy selves, and Father and I will take you and fetch you. Give me the Lamb, dear, and you and Jane put clean lace in your red evening frocks, and I shouldn't wonder if you found they wanted ironing. This paraffin smell is ghastly. Run and get out your frocks."

The frocks did want ironing—wanted it rather badly, as it happened; for, being of tomato-colored Liberty silk, they had been found very useful for *tableaux vivants* when a red dress was required for Cardinal Richelieu. They were very nice *tableaux*, these, and I wish I could tell you about them; but one cannot tell everything in a story. You would have been specially interested in hearing about the *tableaux* of the princes of the tower, when one of the pillows burst, and the youthful princes were so covered with feathers that the picture might very well have been called Michaelmas Eve; or, Plucking the Geese.

Ironing the dresses and sewing the lace in occupied some time, and no one was dull, because there was the theater to look forward to, and also the possible growth of hairs on the carpet, for which everyone kept looking anxiously. By four o'clock Jane was almost sure that several hairs were beginning to grow.

The Phoenix perched on the fender, and its conversation, as usual, was entertaining and instructive—like school prizes are said to be. But it seemed a little absentminded and even a little sad.

"Don't you feel well, Phoenix dear?" asked Anthea, stooping to take an iron off the fire.

"I am not sick," replied the golden bird with a gloomy shake of the head, "but I am getting old."

"Why, you've only been hatched about two months."

"Time," remarked the Phoenix, "is measured by heartbeats. I'm sure the palpitations I've had since I've known you are enough to blanch the feathers of any bird."

"But I thought you lived five hundred years," said Robert, "and you've hardly begun this set of years. Think of all the time that's before you."

"Time," said the Phoenix, "is, as you are probably aware, merely a convenient fiction. There is no such thing as time. I have lived in these two months at a pace which generously counterbalances five hundred years of life in the desert. I am old, I am weary. I feel as if I ought to lay my egg and lay me down to my fiery sleep. But unless I'm careful I shall be hatched again instantly, and that is a misfortune which I really do not think I *could* endure. But do not let me intrude these desperate personal reflections on your youthful happiness. What is the show at the theater tonight? Wrestlers? Gladiators? A combat of tame leopards and unicorns?"

"I don't think so," said Cyril. "It's called *The Water Babies*, and if it's like the book there isn't any gladiating in it. There are chimney sweeps and professors, and a lobster and an otter and a salmon, and children living in the water."

"It sounds chilly." The Phoenix shivered and went to sit on the tongs.

"I don't suppose there will be *real* water," said Jane. "And theaters are very warm and pretty, with a lot of gold and lamps. Wouldn't you like to come with us?"

"*I* was just going to say that," said Robert, in injured tones, "only I know how rude it is to interrupt. Do come, Phoenix, old chap; it will cheer you up. It'll make you laugh like anything. Mr. Bourchier always makes ripping plays. You ought to have seen *Shock-headed Peter* last year."

"Your words are strange," said the Phoenix, "but I will come with you. The revels of this Bourchier, of whom you speak, may help me to forget the weight of my years."

So that evening the Phoenix snugged inside the waistcoat of Robert's Etons—a very tight fit it seemed both to Robert and to the Phoenix—and was taken to the play.

Robert had to pretend to be cold at the glittering, many-mirrored restaurant where they all had dinner, with Father in evening dress, with a very shiny white shirt front, and Mother looking lovely in her gray evening dress, which changes into pink and green when she moves. Robert pretended that he was too cold to take off his greatcoat, and so sat sweltering through what would otherwise have been a most thrilling meal. He felt that he was a blot on the smart beauty of the family, and he hoped the Phoenix knew what he was suffering for its sake. Of course, we are all pleased to suffer for the sake of others, but we like them to know it—unless we were the very best and noblest kind of people, and Robert was just ordinary.

Father was full of jokes and fun, and everyone laughed all the time, even with their mouths full, which is not manners.

Robert thought Father would not have been quite so funny about his keeping his overcoat on if Father had known all the truth. And there Robert was probably right.

When dinner was finished to the last grape and the last paddle in the finger glasses—for it was a really truly grown-up dinner—the children were taken to the theater, guided to a box close to the stage, and left.

Father's parting words were: "Now, don't you stir out of this box, whatever you do. I shall be back before the end of the play. Be good and you will be happy. Is this zone torrid enough for the abandonment of greatcoats, Bobs? No? Well, then, I should say you were sickening for something—mumps or measles or thrush or teething. Good-bye."

He went, and Robert was at last able to remove his coat, mop his perspiring brow, and release the crushed and disheveled Phoenix. Robert had to arrange his damp hair at the looking glass at the back of the box, and the Phoenix had to preen its disordered feathers for some time before either of them was fit to be seen.

They were very, very early. When the lights went up fully, the Phoenix, balancing itself on the gilded back of a chair, swayed in ecstasy.

"How fair a scene is this!" it murmured. "How far fairer than my temple! Or have I guessed aright? Have you brought me hither to lift up my heart with emotions of joyous surprise? Tell me, my Robert, is it not that this, *this* is my true temple, and the other was but a humble shrine frequented by outcasts?"

"I don't know about outcasts," said Robert, "but you can call this your temple if you like. Hush! the music is beginning."

I am not going to tell you about the play. As I said before,

you can't tell everything, and no doubt you saw *The Water
Babies* yourselves. If you did not it was a shame, or rather, a
pity.

What I must tell you is that, though Cyril and Jane and
Robert and Anthea enjoyed it as much as any children
possibly could, the pleasure of the Phoenix was far, far
greater than theirs.

"This is indeed my temple," it said again and again.
"What radiant rites! And all to do honor to me!"

The songs in the play it took to be hymns in its honor.
The choruses were choric songs in its praise. The electric
lights, it said, were magic torches lighted for its sake, and it
was so charmed with the footlights that the children could
hardly persuade it to sit still. But when the limelight was
shown it could contain its approval no longer. It flapped its
golden wings and cried in a voice that could be heard all
over the theater: "Well done, my servants! Ye have my favor
and my countenance!"

Little Tom on the stage stopped short in what he was
saying. A deep breath was drawn by hundreds of lungs, every
eye in the house turned to the box where the luckless
children cringed, and most people hissed, or said "Shish!" or
"Turn them out!"

Then the play went on, and an attendant presently came
to the box and spoke wrathfully.

"It wasn't us, indeed it wasn't," said Anthea earnestly. "It
was the bird."

The man said well, then, they must keep their bird very
quiet.

"Disturbing everyone like this," he said.

"It won't do it again," said Robert, glancing imploringly at the golden bird. "I'm sure it won't."

"You have my leave to depart," said the Phoenix gently.

"Well, he is a beauty, and no mistake," said the attendant, "only I'd cover him up during the acts. It upsets the performance."

And he went.

"Don't speak again, there's a dear," said Anthea. "You wouldn't like to interfere with your own temple, would you?"

So now the Phoenix was quiet, but it kept whispering to the children. It wanted to know why there was no altar, no fire, no incense, and became so excited and fretful and tiresome that four at least of the party of five wished deeply that it had been left at home.

What happened next was entirely the fault of the Phoenix. It was not in the least the fault of the theater people, and no one could ever understand afterward how it did happen. No one, that is, except the guilty bird itself and the four children. The Phoenix was balancing itself on the gilt back of the chair, swaying backward and forward and up and down, as you may see your own domestic parrot do. I mean the gray one with the red tail. All eyes were on the stage, where the lobster was delighting the audience with that gem of a song, "If you can't walk straight, walk sideways!" when the Phoenix murmured:

"No altar, no fire, no incense!" and then, before any of the children could even begin to think of stopping it, it spread its bright wings and swept round the theater, brushing its gleaming feathers against delicate hangings and gilded woodwork.

It seemed to have made but one circular wing-sweep, such

as you may see a gull make over gray water on a stormy day. Next moment it was perched again on the chair back—and all round the theater, where it had passed, little sparks shone like tinsel seeds, then little smoke wreaths curled up like growing plants—little flames opened like flower buds.

People whispered—then people shrieked.

"Fire! Fire!" The curtain went down—the lights went up.

"Fire!" cried everyone, and made for the doors.

"A magnificent idea!" said the Phoenix complacently. "An enormous altar—fire supplied free of charge. Doesn't the incense smell delicious?" The only smell was the stifling smell of smoke, of burning silk, or scorching varnish.

The little flames had opened now into great flame flowers. The people in the theater were shouting and pressing toward the doors.

"Oh, how *could* you!" cried Jane. "Let's get out."

"Father said stay here," said Anthea, very pale and trying to speak in her ordinary voice.

"He didn't mean stay and be roasted," said Robert. "No boys on burning decks for me, thank you."

"Not much," said Cyril, and he opened the door of the box.

But a fierce waft of smoke and hot air made him shut it again. It was not possible to get out that way.

They looked over the front of the box. Could they climb down?

It would be possible, certainly; but would they be much better off?

"Look at the people," Anthea moaned. "We couldn't get through." And, indeed, the crowd round the doors looked thick as flies in the jam-making season.

"I wish we'd never seen the Phoenix," said Jane.

Even at that awful moment Robert looked round to see if the bird had overheard a speech which, however natural, was hardly polite or grateful.

The Phoenix was gone.

"Look here," said Cyril, "I've read about fires in papers; I'm sure it's all right. Let's wait here, as Father said."

"We can't do anything else," said Anthea bitterly.

"Look here," said Robert, "I'm *not* frightened—no, I'm not. The Phoenix has never been a skunk yet, and I'm certain it'll see us through somehow. I believe in the Phoenix."

"The Phoenix thanks you, O Robert," said a golden voice at his feet, and there was the Phoenix itself, on the wishing carpet.

"Quick!" it said. "Stand on those portions of the carpet which are truly antique and authentic—and—"

A sudden jet of flame stopped its words. Alas! the Phoenix had unconsciously warmed to its subject, and in the unintentional heat of the moment had set fire to the paraffin with which that morning the children had anointed the carpet. It burned merrily. The children tried in vain to stamp it out. They had to stand back and let it burn itself out. When the paraffin had burned away it was found that it had taken with it all the darns of Scotch heather mixture fingering. Only the fabric of the old carpet was left—and that was full of holes.

"Come," said the Phoenix, "I'm cool now."

The four children got on to what was left of the carpet. Very careful they were not to leave a leg or a hand hanging over one of the holes. It was very hot—the theater was a pit of fire. Everyone else had got out.

Jane had to sit on Anthea's lap.

"Home!" said Cyril, and instantly the cool draught from under the nursery door played upon their legs as they sat. They were all on the carpet still, and the carpet was lying in its proper place on the nursery floor, as calm and unmoved as though it had never been to the theater or taken part in a fire in its life.

Four long breaths of deep relief were instantly breathed. The draught which they had never liked before was for the moment quite pleasant. And they were safe. And everyone else was safe. The theater had been quite empty when they left. Everyone was sure of that.

They presently found themselves all talking at once. Somehow none of their adventures had given them so much to talk about. None other had seemed so real.

"Did you notice—?" they said, and "Do you remember—?"

When suddenly Anthea's face turned pale under the dirt which it had collected on it during the fire.

"Oh," she cried, "Mother and Father! Oh, how awful! They'll think we're burned to cinders. Oh, let's go this minute and tell them we aren't."

"We should only miss them," said the sensible Cyril.

"Well—*you* go, then," said Anthea, "or I will. Only do wash your face first. Mother will be sure to think you are burnt to a cinder if she sees you as black as that, and she'll faint or be ill or something. Oh, I wish we'd never got to know that Phoenix."

"Hush!" said Robert. "It's no use being rude to the bird. I suppose it can't help its nature. Perhaps we'd better wash too. Now I come to think of it my hands are rather—"

No one had noticed the Phoenix since it had bidden them

to step on the carpet. And no one noticed that no one had noticed.

All were partially clean, and Cyril was just plunging into his greatcoat to go and look for his parents—he, and not unjustly, called it looking for a needle in a bundle of hay—when the sound of Father's latchkey in the front door sent everyone bounding up the stairs.

"Are you all safe?" cried Mother's voice. "Are you all safe?" and the next moment she was kneeling on the linoleum of the hall, trying to kiss four damp children at once, and laughing and crying by turns, while Father stood looking on and saying he was blessed or something.

"But how did you guess we'd come home?" said Cyril, later, when everyone was calm enough for talking.

"Well, it was rather a rum thing. We heard the Garrick was on fire, and of course we went straight there," said Father briskly. "We couldn't find you, of course—and we couldn't get in—but the firemen told us everyone was safely out. And then I heard a voice at my ear say, 'Cyril, Anthea, Robert, and Jane'—and something touched me on the shoulder. It was a great yellow pigeon, and it got in the way of my seeing who'd spoken. It fluttered off, and then someone said in the other ear, 'They're safe at home'; and when I turned again, to see who it was speaking, hanged if there wasn't that confounded pigeon on my other shoulder. Dazed by the fire, I suppose. Your mother said it was the voice of—"

"I said it was the bird that spoke," said Mother, "and so it was. Or at least I thought so then. It wasn't a pigeon. It was an orange-colored cockatoo. I don't care who it was that spoke. It was true—and you're safe."

Mother began to cry again, and Father said bed was a good place after the pleasure of the stage.

So everyone went there.

Robert had a talk to the Phoenix that night.

"Oh, very well," said the bird, when Robert had said what he felt, "didn't you know that I had power over fire? Do not distress yourself. I, like my high priests in Lombard Street, can undo the work of flames. Kindly open the casement."

It flew out.

That was why the papers said next day that the fire at the theater had done less damage than had been anticipated. As a matter of fact it had done none, for the Phoenix spent the night in putting things straight. How the management accounted for this, and how many of the theater officials still believe that they were mad on that night will never be known.

Next day Mother saw the burnt holes in the carpet.

"It caught where it was paraffiny," said Anthea.

"I must get rid of that carpet at once," said Mother.

But what the children said in sad whispers to each other, as they pondered over last night's events, was:

"We must get rid of that Phoenix."

# Chapter 12

# The End of the End

"*E*gg, toast, tea, milk, teacup and saucer, egg spoon, knife, butter—that's all, I think," remarked Anthea, as she put the last touches to Mother's breakfast tray, and went very carefully up the stairs, feeling for every step with her toes and holding on to the tray with all her fingers. She crept into Mother's room and set the tray on the chair. Then she pulled one of the blinds up very softly.

"Is your head better, Mammy dear?" she asked in the soft little voice that she kept expressly for Mother's headaches. "I've brought your brekkie, and I've put the little cloth with the clover leaves on it, the one I made you."

"That's very nice," said Mother sleepily.

Anthea knew exactly what to do for mothers with headaches who had breakfast in bed. She fetched warm water, and put just enough eau de Cologne in it, and bathed Mother's face and hands with the sweet-scented water. Then Mother was able to think about breakfast.

"But what's the matter with my girl?" she asked, when her eyes got used to the light.

"Oh, I'm so sorry you're ill," Anthea said. "It's that horrible fire and you being so frightened. Father said so. And we all feel as if it was our faults. I can't explain, but—"

"It wasn't your fault a bit, you darling goosie," Mother said. "How could it be?"

"That's just what I can't tell you," said Anthea. "I haven't got a futile brain like you and Father, to think of ways of explaining everything."

Mother laughed.

"My futile brain—or did you mean fertile?—anyway, it feels very stiff and sore this morning—but I shall be quite all right by-and-by. And don't be a silly little girl. The fire wasn't your faults. No; I don't want the egg, dear. I'll go to sleep again, I think. Don't you worry. And tell Cook not to bother me about meals. You can order what you like for lunch."

Anthea closed the door very mousily, and instantly went downstairs and ordered what she liked for lunch. She ordered a pair of turkeys, a large plum pudding, cheesecakes, and almonds and raisins.

Cook told her to go along, do. And she might as well not have ordered anything, for when lunch came it was just hashed mutton and semolina pudding, and Cook had forgotten the sippets for the mutton hash, and the semolina pudding was burnt.

When Anthea rejoined the others she found them all plunged in the gloom where she was herself. For everyone knew that the days of the carpet were now numbered. Indeed, so worn was it that you could almost have numbered its threads.

So that now, after nearly a month of magic happenings,

the time was at hand when life would have to go on in the dull, ordinary way, and Jane, Robert, Anthea, and Cyril would be just in the same position as the other children who live in Camden Town, the children whom these four had so often pitied, and perhaps a little despised.

"We shall be just like that," Cyril said.

"Except," said Robert, "that we shall have more things to remember and be sorry we haven't got."

"Mother's going to send away the carpet as soon as she's well enough to see about that coconut matting. Fancy *us* with coconut matting—us! And we've walked under live coconut trees on the island where you can't have whooping cough."

"Pretty island," said the Lamb. "Paint box sands and sea all shiny sparkly."

His brothers and sisters had often wondered whether he remembered that island. Now they knew that he did.

"Yes," said Cyril. "No more cheap return trips by carpet for us—that's a dead cert!"

They were all talking about the carpet, but what they were all thinking about was the Phoenix.

The golden bird had been so kind, so friendly, so polite, so instructive—and now it had set fire to a theater and made Mother ill. Nobody blamed the bird. It had acted in a perfectly natural manner. But everyone saw that it must not be asked to prolong its visit. Indeed, in plain English, it must be asked to go!

The four children felt like base spies and trecherous friends; and each in its mind was saying who ought not to be the one to tell the Phoenix that there could no longer be a place for it in that happy home in Camden Town. Each child was quite sure that one of them ought to speak out in a fair and manly way, but nobody wanted to be the one.

They could not talk the whole thing over as they would have liked to do, because the Phoenix itself was in the cupboard, among the blackbeetles and the odd shoes and the broken chessmen.

But Anthea tried.

"It's very horrid. I do hate thinking things about people, and not being able to say the things you're thinking because of the way they would feel when they thought what things you were thinking, and wondered what they'd done to make you think things like that, and why you were thinking them."

Anthea was so anxious that the Phoenix should not understand what she said that she made a speech completely baffling to all. It was not till she pointed out the cupboard in which all believed the Phoenix to be that even Cyril understood.

"Yes," he said, while Jane and Robert were trying to tell each other how deeply they didn't understand what Anthea was saying. "But after recent eventfulness a new leaf has to be turned over, and, after all, Mother is more important than the feelings of any of the lower forms of creation, however unnatural."

"How beautifully you do do it," said Anthea, absently beginning to build a card-house for the Lamb. "Mixing up what you're saying, I mean. We ought to practice doing it so as to be ready for mysterious occasions. We're talking about *that*," she said to Jane and Robert, frowning, and nodding toward the cupboard where the Phoenix was. Then Robert and Jane understood, and each opened its mouth to speak.

"Wait a minute," said Anthea quickly. "The game is to twist up what you want to say so that no one can understand what you're saying except the people you want to understand it, and sometimes not them."

"The ancient philosophers," said a golden voice, "well understood the art of which you speak."

Of course it was the Phoenix, who had not been in the cupboard at all but had been cocking a golden eye at them from the cornice during the whole conversation.

"Pretty dickie!" remarked the Lamb. "*Canary* dickie!"

"Poor, misguided infant," said the Phoenix.

There was a painful pause; the four could not but think it likely that the Phoenix had understood their very veiled allusions, accompanied as they had been by gestures indicating the cupboard. For the Phoenix was not wanting in intelligence.

"We were just saying—" Cyril began, and I hope he was not going to say anything but the truth. Whatever it was he did not say it, for the Phoenix interrupted him, and all breathed more freely as it spoke.

"I gather," it said, "that you have some tidings of a fatal nature to communicate to our degraded black brothers who run to and fro forever yonder."

It pointed a claw at the cupboard, where the blackbeetles lived.

"Canary *talk*," said the Lamb joyously. "Go and show Mammy."

He wriggled off Anthea's lap.

"Mammy's asleep," said Jane hastily. "Come and be wild beasts in a cage under the table."

But the Lamb caught his feet and hands, and even his

head, so often and so deeply in the holes of the carpet that the cage, or table, had to be moved onto the linoleum, and the carpet lay bare to sight with all its horrid holes.

"Ah," said the bird, "it isn't long for this world."

"No," said Robert, "everything comes to an end. It's awful."

"Sometimes the end is peace," remarked the Phoenix. "I imagine that unless it comes soon, the end of your carpet will be pieces."

"Yes," said Cyril, respectfully kicking what was left of the carpet. The movement of its bright colors caught the eye of the Lamb, who went down on all fours instantly and began to pull at the red and blue threads.

"Aggedydaggedygaggedy," murmured the Lamb. "Daggedy ag ag ag!"

And before anyone could have winked (even if they had wanted to, and it would not have been of the slightest use) the middle of the floor showed bare an island of boards surrounded by a sea of linoleum. The magic carpet was gone, *and so was the Lamb!*

There was a horrible silence. The Lamb—the baby, all alone—had been wafted away on that untrustworthy carpet, so full of holes and magic. And no one could know where he was. And no one could follow him because there was now no carpet to follow on.

Jane burst into tears, but Anthea, though pale and frantic, was dry-eyed.

"It *must* be a dream," she said.

"That's what the clergyman said," remarked Robert forlornly. "But it wasn't, and it isn't."

"But the Lamb never wished," said Cyril. "He was only talking Bosh."

"The carpet understands all speech," said the Phoenix, "even Bosh. I know not this Boshland, but be assured that its tongue is not unknown to the carpet."

"Do you mean, then," said Anthea, in white terror, "that when he was saying 'Aggety dag,' or whatever it was, he meant something by it?"

"All speech has meaning," said the Phoenix.

"There I think you're wrong," said Cyril. "Even people who talk English sometimes say things that don't mean anything in particular."

"Oh, never mind that now," Anthea moaned. "You think 'Aggety dag' meant something to him and the carpet?"

"Beyond doubt it held the same meaning to the carpet as to the luckless infant," the Phoenix said calmly.

"And *what* did it mean? Oh, *what?*"

"Unfortunately," the bird rejoined, "I never studied Bosh."

Jane sobbed noisily, but the others were calm with what is sometimes called the calmness of despair. The Lamb was gone—the Lamb, their own precious baby brother—who had never in his happy little life been for a moment out of the sight of eyes that loved him—he was gone. He had gone alone into the great world with no other companion and protector than a carpet with holes in it. The children had never really understood before what an enormously big place the world is. And the Lamb might be anywhere in it!

"And it's no use going to look for him." Cyril, in flat and wretched tones, only said what the others were thinking.

"Do you wish him to return?" the Phoenix asked; it seemed to speak with some surprise.

"Of course we do," cried everybody.

"Isn't he more trouble than he's worth?" asked the bird doubtfully.

"No, no. Oh, we do want him back! We do!"

"Then," said the wearer of gold plumage, "if you'll excuse me, I'll just pop out and see what I can do."

Cyril flung open the window, and the Phoenix popped out.

"Oh, if only Mother goes on sleeping! Oh, suppose she wakes up and wants the Lamb! Oh, suppose the servants come! Stop crying, Jane. It's no earthly good. No, I'm not crying myself—at least I wasn't till you said so, and I shouldn't anyway if—if there was any mortal thing we could do. Oh, oh, oh!"

Cyril and Robert were boys, and boys never cry, of course. Still, the position was a terrible one, and I do not wonder that they made faces in their efforts to behave in a really manly way.

And at this awful moment Mother's bell rang.

A breathless stillness held the children. Then Anthea dried her eyes. She looked round her and caught up the poker. She held it out to Cyril.

"Hit my hand hard," she said. "I must show Mother some reason for my eyes being like they are. Harder," she cried as Cyril gently tapped her with the iron handle. And Cyril, agitated and trembling, nerved himself to hit harder, and hit very much harder than he intended.

Anthea screamed.

"Oh, Panther, I didn't mean to hurt, really," cried Cyril, clattering the poker back into the fender.

"It's—all—right," said Anthea breathlessly, clasping the

hurt hand with the one that wasn't hurt. "It's—getting—red."

It was—a round red and blue bump was rising on the back of it.

"Now, Robert," she said, trying to breathe more evenly, "you go out—oh, I don't know where—on to the dustbin—anywhere—and I shall tell Mother you and the Lamb are out."

Anthea was now ready to deceive her mother for as long as ever she could. Deceit is very wrong, we know, but it seemed to Anthea that it was her plain duty to keep her mother from being frightened about the Lamb as long as possible. And the Phoenix *might* help.

"It always has helped," Robert said. "It got us out of the tower, and even when it made the fire in the theater it got us out all right. I'm certain it will manage somehow."

Mother's bell rang again.

"Oh, Eliza's never answered it," cried Anthea. "She never does. Oh, I must go."

And she went.

Her heart beat bumpingly as she climbed the stairs. Mother would be certain to notice her eyes—well, her hand would account for that. But the Lamb—

"No, I must *not* think of the Lamb," she said to herself, and bit her tongue till her eyes watered again, so as to give herself something else to think of. Her arms and legs and back, and even her tear-reddened face, felt stiff with her resolution not to let Mother be worried if she could help it.

She opened the door softly.

"Yes, Mother?" she said.

"Dearest," said Mother, "the Lamb—"

Anthea tried to be brave. She tried to say that the Lamb and Robert were out. Perhaps she tried too hard. Anyway, when she opened her mouth no words came. So she stood with it open. It seemed easier to keep from crying with one's mouth in that position.

"The Lamb," Mother went on. "He was very good at first, but he's pulled the toilet cover off the dressing table with all the brushes and pots and things, and now he's so quiet I'm sure he's in some dreadful mischief. And I can't see him from here, and if I'd got out of bed to see I'm sure I should have fainted."

"Do you mean he's *here?*" said Anthea.

"Of course he's here," said Mother a little impatiently. "Where did you think he was?"

Anthea went round the foot of the big mahogany bed. There was a pause.

"He's not here *now*," she said.

That he had been there was plain, from the toilet cover on the floor, the scattered pots and bottles, the wandering brushes and combs, all involved in the tangle of ribbons and laces which an open drawer had yielded to the baby's inquisitive fingers.

"He must have crept out then," said Mother. "Do keep him with you, there's a darling. If I don't get some sleep I shall be a wreck when Father comes home."

Anthea closed the door softly. Then she tore downstairs and burst into the nursery, crying:

"He must have wished he was with Mother. He's been there all the time, 'Aggety dag—'"

The unusual word was frozen on her lip, as people say in books.

For there, on the floor, lay the carpet, and on the carpet, surrounded by his brothers and by Jane, sat the Lamb. He had covered his face and clothes with Vaseline and violet powder, but he was easily recognizable in spite of his disguise.

"You are right," said the Phoenix, who was also present. "It is evident that, as you say, 'Aggety dag' is Bosh for 'I want to be where my mother is,' and so the faithful carpet understood it."

"But how," said Anthea, catching up the Lamb and hugging him, "how did he get back here?"

"Oh," said the Phoenix, "I flew to the Psammead and wished that your infant brother were restored to your midst, and immediately it was so."

"Oh, I am glad, I am glad," cried Anthea, still hugging the baby. "Oh, you darling! Shut up, Jane! I don't care *how* much he comes off on me! Cyril! You and Robert roll that carpet up and put it in the beetle cupboard. He might say 'Aggety dag' again, and it might mean something quite different next time. Now, my Lamb, Panther'll clean you a little. Come on."

"I hope the beetles won't go wishing," said Cyril, as they rolled up the carpet.

Two days later Mother was well enough to go out, and that evening the coconut matting came home. The children had talked and talked, and thought and thought, but they had not found any polite way of telling the Phoenix that they did not want it to stay any longer.

The days had been days spent by the children in embarrassment, and by the Phoenix in sleep.

And, now the matting was laid down, the Phoenix awoke and fluttered down onto it.

It shook its crested head.

"I like not this carpet," it said. "It is harsh and unyielding, and it hurts my golden feet."

"We've jolly well got to get used to its hurting *our* golden feet," said Cyril.

"This, then," said the bird, "supersedes the wishing carpet."

"Yes," said Robert, "if you mean that it's instead of it."

"And the magic web?" inquired the Phoenix, with sudden eagerness.

"It's the rag-and-bottle man's day tomorrow," said Anthea in a low voice. "He will take it away."

The Phoenix fluttered up to its favorite perch on the chair back.

"Hear me!" it cried. "Oh youthful children of men, and restrain your tears of misery and despair, for what must be must be, and I would not remember you, thousands of years hence, as base ingrates and crawling worms compact of low selfishness."

"I should hope not, indeed," said Cyril.

"Weep not," the bird went on. "I really do beg that you won't weep. I will not seek to break the news to you gently. Let the blow fall at once. The time has come when I must leave you."

All four children breathed forth a long sigh of relief.

"We needn't have bothered so about how to break the news to it," whispered Cyril.

"Ah, sigh not so," said the bird gently. "All meetings end in partings. I must leave you. I have sought to prepare you for this. Ah, do not give way!"

"Must you really go—so soon?" murmured Anthea. It was what she had often heard her mother say to calling ladies in the afternoon.

"I must, really; thank you so much, dear," replied the bird, just as though it had been one of the ladies.

"I am weary," it went on. "I desire to rest—after all the happenings of this last moon I do desire greatly to rest, and I ask of you one last boon."

"Any little thing we can do," said Robert.

Now that it had really come to parting with the Phoenix, whose favorite he had always been, Robert did feel almost as miserable as the Phoenix thought they all did.

"I ask but the relic designed for the rag-and-bottle man. Give me what is left of the carpet and let me go."

"Dare we?" said Anthea. "Would Mother mind?"

"I have dared greatly for your sakes," remarked the bird.

"Well, then, we will," said Robert.

The Phoenix fluffed out its feathers joyously.

"Nor shall you regret it, children of golden hearts," it said. "Quick—spread the carpet and leave me alone; but first pile high the fire. Then, while I am immersed in the sacred preliminary rites, do ye prepare sweet-smelling woods and spices for the last act of parting."

The children spread out what was left of the carpet. And, after all, though this was just what they would have wished to have happened, all hearts were sad. Then they put half a scuttle of coal on the fire and went out, closing the door on the Phoenix—left, at last, alone with the carpet.

"One of us must keep watch," said Robert excitedly, as soon as they were all out of the room, "and the others can go and buy sweet woods and spices. Get the very best that money can buy, and plenty of them. Don't let's stand to a threepence or so. I want it to have a jolly good send-off. It's the only thing that'll make us feel less horrid inside."

It was felt that Robert, as the pet of the Phoenix, ought to have the last melancholy pleasure of choosing the materials for its funeral pyre.

"I'll keep watch if you like," said Cyril. "I don't mind. And, besides, it's raining hard, and my boots let in the wet. You might call and see if my other ones are 'really reliable' again yet."

So they left Cyril, standing like a Roman sentinel outside the door inside which the Phoenix was getting ready for the great change, and they all went out to buy the precious things for the last sad rites.

"Robert is right," Anthea said. "This is no time for being careful about our money. Let's go to the stationer's first and buy a whole packet of lead pencils. They're cheaper if you buy them by the packet."

This was a thing that they had always wanted to do, but it needed the great excitement of a funeral pyre and a parting from a beloved Phoenix to screw them up to the extravagance.

The people at the stationer's said that the pencils were real cedar-wood, so I hope they were, for stationers should always speak the truth. At any rate they cost one-and-fourpence. Also they spent sevenpence three farthings on a little sandalwood box inlaid with ivory.

"Because," said Anthea, "I know sandalwood smells sweet, and when it's burned I expect it smells very sweet indeed."

"Ivory doesn't smell at all," said Robert, "but I expect when you burn it it smells most awful vile, like bones."

At the grocer's they bought all the spices they could

remember the names of—shell-like mace; cloves like blunt
nails; peppercorns, the long and the round kind; ginger, the
dry sort, of course; and beautiful bloom-covered shells of
fragrant cinnamon. Allspice too, and caraway seeds (caraway
seeds that smelled most deadly when the time came for
burning them).

Camphor and oil of lavender were brought at the chemist's
and also a little scent sachet labeled "Violettes de Parme."

The took the things home and found Cyril still on guard.
When they had knocked and the golden voice of the Phoenix
had said, "Come in," they went in.

There lay the carpet—or what was left of it—and on it lay
an egg, exactly like the one out of which the Phoenix had
been hatched.

The Phoenix was walking round and round the egg, cluck-
ing with joy and pride.

"I've laid it, you see," it said, "and as fine an egg as ever I
laid in all my born days."

Everyone said yes, it was indeed a beauty.

The things which the children had bought were now
taken out of their papers and arranged on the table, and
when the Phoenix had been persuaded to leave its egg for a
moment and look at the materials for its last fire it was quite
overcome.

"Never, never have I had a finer pyre than this will be.
You shall not regret it," it said, wiping away a golden tear.
"Write quickly: 'Go and tell the Psammead to fulfill the last
wish of the Phoenix, and return instantly.' "

But Robert wished to be polite and he wrote:

"Please go and ask the Psammead to be so kind as to fulfill

the Phoenix's last wish, and come straight back, if you please."

The paper was pinned to the carpet, which vanished and returned in the flash of an eye.

Then another paper was written ordering the carpet to take the egg somewhere where it wouldn't be hatched for another two thousand years. The Phoenix tore itself away from its cherished egg, which it watched with yearning tenderness till, the paper being pinned on, the carpet hastily rolled itself up round the egg, and both vanished forever from the nursery of the house in Camden Town.

"Oh, dear! Oh, dear! Oh, dear!" said everybody.

"Bear up," said the bird. "Do you think I don't suffer, being parted from my precious new-laid egg like this? Come, conquer your emotions and build my fire."

"*Oh!*" cried Robert suddenly, and wholly breaking down. "I can't *bear* you to go!"

The Phoenix perched on his shoulder and rubbed his beak softly against his ear.

"The sorrows of youth soon appear but as dreams," it said. "Farewell, Robert of my heart. I have loved you well."

The fire had burnt to a red glow. One by one the spices and sweet woods were laid on it. Some smelled nice and some—the caraway seeds and the Violettes de Parme sachet among them—smelled worse than you would think possible.

"Farewell, farewell, farewell, farewell!" said the Phoenix in a faraway voice.

"Oh, *good-bye*," said everyone, and now all were in tears.

The bright bird fluttered seven times round the room and settled in the hot heart of the fire. The sweet gums and spices and woods flared and flickered around it, but its

golden feathers did not burn. It seemed to grow red-hot to
the very inside heart of it—and then before the eight eyes of
its friends it fell together, a heap of white ashes, and the
flames of the cedar pencils and the sandalwood box met and
joined above it.

"Whatever have you done with the carpet?" asked Mother
next day.

"We gave it to someone who wanted it very much. The
name began with a P," said Jane. The others instantly
hushed her.

"Oh, well, it wasn't worth twopence," said Mother.

"The person who began with P said we shouldn't lose by
it," Jane went on before she could be stopped.

"I daresay!" said Mother, laughing.

But that very night a great box came, addressed to the
children by all their names. Eliza never could remember the
name on the carrier who brought it. It wasn't Carter Paterson
or the Parcels Delivery.

It was instantly opened. It was a big wooden box, and it
had to be opened with a hammer and the kitchen poker; the
long nails came squeaking out, and the boards scrunched as
they were wrenched off. Inside the box was soft paper, with
beautiful Chinese patterns on it—blue and green and red and
violet. And under the paper—well, almost everything lovely
that you can think of. Everything of reasonable size, I mean;
for, of course, there were no motor cars or flying machines or
Thoroughbred chargers. But there really was almost everything else. Everything that the children had always wanted—
toys and games and books, and chocolate and candied cherries
and paintboxes and photographic cameras, and all the pres-

ents they had always wanted to give to Father and Mother and the Lamb, only they had never had the money for them. At the very bottom of the box was a tiny golden feather. No one saw it but Robert, and he picked it up and hid it in the breast of his jacket, which had been so often the nesting place of the golden bird. When he went to bed the feather was gone. It was the last he ever saw of the Phoenix.

Pinned to the lovely fur cloak that mother had always wanted was a paper, and it said:

"In return for the carpet. With gratitude. —P."

You may guess how Father and Mother talked it over. They decided at last that the person who had had the carpet, and whom, curiously enough, the children were quite unable to describe, must be an insane millionaire who amused himself by playing at being a rag-and-bone man. But the children knew better.

They knew that this was the fulfillment, by the powerful Psammead, of the last wish of the Phoenix, and that this glorious and delightful boxful of treasures was really the very, very, very end of the Phoenix and the Carpet.

# Afterword

# Susan Cooper

*M*y favorite line in *The Phoenix and the Carpet* comes at the end of the episode about the queen-cook. It reads: "The story is indeed a little difficult to believe. Still, you might try."

It was written out of great confidence, that line. E. Nesbit knew very well that anybody who had read that far was a total believer, and would have no trouble at all in accepting the translation of a dumpy middle-aged lady from cook to queen. She hooked me when I was your age, and she hooks me now as adult all over again; she makes me believe that magical events can take place *in real life*. It's the incongruity of the mixture that's so marvelous: the egg of a mythical bird hatching in an ordinary London fireplace; four sturdily ordinary children taking off on a flying, wish-granting carpet through space and time. A gray, dull world is suddenly brilliant with possibilities; who knows *what* will happen next?

I still have trouble with those children, I have to tell you. I thought they were Victorian fossils when I was young, and I still do. Cyril, Anthea, Robert, and Jane have never a rebellious word to say to their beautiful fragile mother or their manly upright father, but they are coolly condescending to the invariably self-centered, untrustworthy servants. Cyril, Anthea, Robert, and Jane (and probably the baby too) are, I regret to say, middle-class English snobs. They are also classically sexist: the boys expect the girls to do the dishes and mend the carpet when necessary, and the girls do it uncomplaining. Boys can be boys, but girls have to be little women.

Of course it doesn't matter, really. Such things go with the territory, in a Victorian "children's book," like the old-fashioned clothes on the cover, the dated slang ("I say, old chap! How ripping!") and the blandly racist assumption that tropical islands are inhabited by "copper-colored savages." Once the story begins to roll, we forget our quibbles, because those children are *real*, in spite of their flounces and knicker-bockers. They slip out of their nineteenth-century aura and suddenly there they are, clear and alive, feeling and behaving just like people we know.

And I sometimes catch myself wondering whether E. Nesbit might not have had a certain hidden contempt for Victorian ladies like Mother, who turns pale when the cook threatens to leave, and agrees with Father's opinion about almost anything "because mothers have to agree with fathers, and not because it was her own idea." Mother, we are told, "was really a great dear. She was pretty and she was loving, and most frightfully good when you were ill, and always kind, and almost always just." (The "almost" is a relief.) In fact she hasn't much excuse to be anything else, since Father packs her off to the seaside when she merely catches a cold, and she is never in danger of anything so vulgar as employment. Perhaps E. Nesbit is inserting a small needle-sharp comment on Mother when she writes of the school bazaar stall stocked with "table covers and mats and things embroidered beautifully *by idle ladies with no real work to do*" (my italics). Or then again, perhaps she has Mother dispatched to the idle seaside simply as an author's convenience. It's undeniably easier for the children to have adventures with phoenixes and carpets if Father is off at work and Mother is off on a distant beach. . . .

There was nothing idle about E. Nesbit herself. She had an extraordinary and unconventional private life and wrote dozens of novels, short stories, articles, and poems, supporting her husband and family for most of her life. A lot of her readers thought "E. Nesbit" must be a man—including H. G. Wells, who became so convinced that her name ought to be Ernest that his letters to her went on beginning "Dear Ernest" for years after they had met one another and become friends. Together with Shakespeare, Lord Nelson, and Walter de la Mare, Edith/Ernest is high on my list of departed people I wish I could have met.

*The Phoenix and the Carpet, Five Children and It* (which is even better), and *The Story of the Amulet* are the only fantasies I remember reading when I was a child; my other favorites were the firmly realistic adventures of the English novelists Arthur Ransome and Malcolm Saville. When I grew up, like E. Nesbit I decided to make my living as a writer; like her, I started in journalism. I'd been a reporter for five years when Ernest Benn, Limited, who had always published her books in England, announced the E. Nesbit Prize, to be awarded for "a family adventure story." I couldn't resist trying this, so I began writing what I thought was a family adventure story—until I found magic creeping in. It was a Nesbit kind of magic, the kind that blossoms astonishingly in the middle of real life and can leave its reader—and perhaps its writer—with an echoing thought: "Who knows, maybe that could happen to me . . ." But the magic stopped my book from being a "family adventure," so I didn't enter it for the prize, and *Over Sea, Under Stone* was published elsewhere. What I didn't know at the time was that this first book would lead to a whole group of related fantasies called *The Dark Is Rising*—and all because of E. Nesbit. If I hadn't written those books, I shouldn't be discussing the phoenix with you here. Everything goes in a circle.

Thank you, Ernest.